All to Herself

Lori Bell

This book is a work of fiction. Names, characters, places and incidents are the product of the author's imagination or are used fictitiously. Any resemblance to actual events, locales, or persons, living or dead, is coincidental.

Cover photograph by CanStock Photo

Printed by CreateSpace

ISBN 978 1729166000

DEDICATION

To the people who have walked into our lives,
and suddenly we can't remember how we ever lived
without them.

In loving memory of Tim Marks
July 14, 1979 – November 12, 2018

Chapter 1

Bent down to his knees on the concrete driveway, Tucker Brandt opened his arms to the tiny-framed blue-eyed little girl he called his own. Livy snuggled against his chest as Tucker tightened his arms around her. He kissed the top of her head, and took a moment to inhale the scent of her hair. She was three and half years old, still merely a baby. She didn't fully understand what was happening, and fortunately she most likely would not remember it in detail.

"Be really good for your mommy, you hear?" Tucker watched her nod her little blonde head. She was a mini replica of her mother. "And I will see you in just a few days."

"Then you're coming to our new house to live?" Livy asked. And her innocence panged his heart.

Tucker carefully shook his head. He was afraid to jostle his noggin too wildly in fear of freeing the tears welling up in his eyes. "No, baby girl. This is still going to be my house, right here," he motioned at the modest ranch-style red brick home behind them. "You will have two houses to live in, your new one with mommy, and this one with me." A part of Tucker wished his daughter had been at an age where change felt threatening to her, so she would adamantly refuse to leave the familiarity of their home. Instead, she would go wherever her mommy wanted, and come back to visit her daddy. Everything was going to change. Even though Tucker was keeping the house after the divorce, it still would not be the same. Living there alone was going to be an adjustment he dreaded. All of his wife's belongings would be gone, and only some of his daughter's things would remain. The silence. The loneliness. Even still, Tucker didn't want to relocate. He chose not to leave there. Because he wanted that house —their home— to be a constant for his daughter. And himself.

"I'll miss you, daddy, when you're here and I'm not." She was smart, and already wise beyond her years it seemed. A tiny old soul, as Tucker liked to say. And right now, her innocence and raw honesty would have easily brought him to his knees had he not already been on them. Even through denim, he could feel the rough concrete piercing his knee caps. He welcomed the discomfort as a distraction for his greater pain.

"Hand over your heart," Tucker told her in a pretend stern voice, as she mimicked his actions and placed her small hand over her chest. Her eyes bore into her daddy's and she smiled wide at him because she knew what he was going to say. "We never really will be apart, because I'm in there," Tucker tapped two of his fingers overtop of her hand. "I'm in your heart, Livy."

"And you're in mine, daddy." It was scripted. They had said that to each other for weeks now, leading up to this day. Tucker heard his older brother clear his throat. This was heavy stuff. Enough to make a grown man fall apart. Chase was outside on the driveway helping to load the last of the things in the back of the SUV that Kate was driving. He was there to support his brother. Kate was on that driveway too. But Tucker never paid any mind to having an audience. This was his moment with his little girl. It was their goodbye to life as they knew it. Not to each other, but to their unity as a family. Kate walked up to them. In skinny jeans and straw-colored wedges, she towered them both still on the ground. Tucker stood, with his daughter now in his arms.

Their eyes met. Livy stayed quiet. It was as if she knew, she could sense the finality of this moment between her parents. Kate flipped her long blonde hair off her shoulder and it fell halfway down her back. Her makeup was flawless. It was obvious she had no concerns about her mascara running today. Unlike Tucker's, her eyes were dry.

"It's like ripping off a band-aid Tucker, you have to just do it quickly." Her words unnerved him. He wanted to ask Kate if that's what she had done, if that was how she handled the fact that their marriage had come undone. *Just feel the heartache for a split second, and then move on.*

"Have Uncle Chase buckle you in and I'll be right there to give you send-off kisses." Livy did as she was told once Tucker placed her feet on the ground.

"You will see her in two days," Kate spoke immediately. "Don't put the idea in her head that she should be sad."

"Maybe she should be?" Tucker fired back with honest thoughts. "If she misses me, I want to know about it. And if she needs me—" Tucker choked on his words, and Kate put her hand to his chest.

"I will, Tucker," she reassured him. "We are going to have this co-parenting thing down in no time." She attempted a smile, but Tucker didn't share her positivity. He was not okay with this, but Kate had a new life waiting for her. A new man. A house more innovative and considerably larger than the one they shared for the past five years. But their house, and everything else, had not been enough. Tucker had not been enough for her.

He didn't know what else to say to his wife. Kate Brandt was still his wife. But not for long. And it was too late to try to alter her plans. It was not as if Tucker expected a change of heart from her. He had just wished she had a heart. It was obvious to him here and now that his was the only one breaking.

"I hope you'll be happy, Kate," Tucker said as he ceased eye contact with her and walked to the open backseat door to kiss his daughter goodbye.

When the black SUV, tinted windows and all, rolled in reverse off the driveway, Tucker stood near his brother. Neither one said a word until Kate drove off.

"You okay?" Chase asked, turning to his younger brother who he stood only an inch taller than.

"That's a dumb question," Tucker responded, still staring down the road.

"It is," Chase agreed, "but it's an important one. She broke your heart, and severed your little family. Don't let her take anything more from you." Tucker creased his brow, as if he needed more of an explanation to understand his brother's words. "You are still you. A man who would do pretty much anything for anyone. You tried to make her happy, you gave her what most women need. Stand tall. You didn't fail. She just gave up."

Tucker nodded. "Thanks for the pep talk."

"Want to grab a beer?" Tucker shook his head to decline the offer. "You're a free man now. You can do those kinds of things again."

"What? Get drunk and pick up women?"

"You're a quick learner," Chase smirked.

Tucker chuckled, even though that attitude was not his style.

They stared off and shared silence. Chase was preparing to leave. Tucker had to go back inside to face his now empty house. Nothing left in there was his and hers anymore. Only his.

"The For Sale sign is down over there," Chase noted, in reference to the house directly across the street.

"Yeah, someone moved in about two or three weeks ago. Kate said she is pretty much all to herself. They met briefly when Livy was playing out in the yard and the neighbor lady was getting the mail or something."

"So, a woman lives there alone? How old? Is she hot?" Chase inquired.

"No idea. I've only seen her in her car, driving up or driving off. I can pay closer attention next time if you're looking?"

Chase shoved him back. He was happily married for the last decade, and had no reason to be looking.

"Go on. Go home. I'll be fine."

"Yes, you will."

Tucker let his big brother pull him into a tight embrace. He shut his eyes for a moment. *He would be alright. It was just going to take time.*

Chapter 2

"Remi?"

Remi Jasper looked up from her laptop on the desk in front of her. Aside from that desk, her office had two chairs and a filing cabinet (that she questioned if anyone else adequately used anymore) crammed into a space which could have been better served as a closet.

"Crue, you're supposed to call me Miss Jasper," Remi tried not to smirk, but the senior at O'Fallon Township High School who entered her office had a charismatic personality that would no doubt take him places in his life.

"Sorry," he replied, but they both knew he didn't sincerely mean it.

"Sit," she said, and he did without hesitation. His faded denim was ripped at the knees and he wore brown leather flip flops on his feet. There were troubled young adults in every high school building. If Crue was struggling with his parents' recent divorce, no one else had picked up on it. Even still, it was Remi's job as the guidance counselor to help where she was needed. She just wasn't exactly sure yet why Crue had insisted on coming to see her once a week since the school year started. Including now, this was already his third session with Remi. "So how are classes?"

"A bore," he stated.

"How's living with your dad going?"

"Well." Remi believed she saw honesty in his eyes. She was in her element, connecting with students. This wasn't a classroom. This was a place where students were not pressured and could let their guard down. Remi knew that Crue and his father had bonded since his parents divorced and his mother checked herself into rehab for her decade-spanned alcohol addiction. The serious issues inside the homes of young people sometimes astounded Remi and compelled her to act. It was the reason she chose counseling as her profession. It didn't make her wealthy, but her career fulfilled her in ways she never imagined when she was able to help children. Technically the high school students she worked with were addressed as young adults, but many were not yet capable of reaching that level of maturity. Crue, however, was.

"So, you tell me then, why are you back here? I thought we decided that you had a good handle on things." Remi previously told him that her office door would always be open. His name on her sign-up list today had surprised her though. There were gaps in her schedule all day long, which she intentionally left open for the students who wanted or needed to talk to her. Her only expectation was they had to be prepared and willing to open up to her. She wasn't a fan of time wasted. In every impromptu session, Remi rarely began with questions of her own. And she initiated each of those sessions the same way with every student — *tell me what's on your mind.*

"My dad is seeing someone, a woman I know actually." Remi placed her elbows on the desktop. Crue had her undivided attention. "I think it's just about sex, well for him at least." Remi kept her composure. Teens and sex were not an uncomfortable subject for her at all. "It's just awkward for me to be around her."

"Does she hang out with both you and your dad?" Remi would be surprised at that. It seemed too premature to involve a child in a dating relationship, especially a teenager. Even more awkward for him, she thought.

"No, just my dad. I only see her in passing." Remi nodded. "It's during sixth hour American History when I'm forced to spend time with her."

"What?" Remi spoke, just as her mind clearly focused on the fact that this was the sixth-class hour of the school day and Crue was supposed to be present in American History, taught by Rhonda Pilgreen. She was thirty-something and single. And for a moment, just out of pure curiosity, Remi wished she knew what Crue's father looked like, so she could pair him up in her mind with Miss Pilgreen to speculate if they looked like a good match. But Remi was new to this school district and unfamiliar with almost everyone in the community. In the school building, however, she already had become acquainted with most of her coworkers in recent weeks.

Crue watched her eyes, and he realized Remi understood. "The first twenty minutes of her class are discussion. The last half we work on our own." He didn't want to be at school in the presence of a woman he had seen practically naked in the privacy of his own home, wearing only his father's shirt.

"Are you asking me for twenty minutes of my time at the start of every American History class? Crue…"

"Before you say you can't, that it's against the rules, or I'll be taking up some other needy kid's spot, just think on it," Crue practically pleaded with her. "You have to admit, it's brilliant."

Remi smiled. "You're brilliant." And he was. He most likely would be the high-ranking valedictorian of his class, and missing those minutes of American History for the entire semester would hardly hurt him.

"Does that mean you'll help me?" Crue all but held his breath awaiting her answer.

"You have to call me Miss Jasper. You must report to me on time and make good use of your twenty minutes. If you don't have anything to say to me, you'll do homework. Got it?"

Crue smiled wide. "Thank you, Miss Jasper." Remi shook her head at the victorious look on his face, and then she laughed out loud. She had a weakness for kids who came from broken homes. As she too was a product of one.

∞∞

Remi pulled into the driveway of her new home. It wasn't just-built brand new, but it was new to her. The cul-de-sac was safe and fairly quiet. There were retired couples and a few young families. Remi had met the woman and her daughter directly across the street. She already thought of the blonde Kate as high maintenance and perhaps somewhat phony, but she had an adorable little girl (whose name she remembered as Livy). Remi had yet to meet the husband. Being as communicative as she had to be all day long at school was enough for her. On her own time, she wanted to be alone. She preferred to keep her personal life all to herself now. It was just easier that way.

Just months after her own parents divorced when she was eleven years old, Remi's father abandoned her. She hadn't seen or spoken to him since. It was as if he vanished and no one cared to try to find him. Remi had at least convinced herself over the years that she had no desire to chase him down and forge a relationship again. Remi's mother was in and out of her adult life, but she never had acted much better than her father who ran away. She jumped from job to job and man to man. Remi had very little respect for her mother's life's choices – or her as a person.

She wanted a better life for herself than what her parents had. She worked hard to find success in her career, and she was proud of her own accomplishments the last eight years following college. O'Fallon Township High School in O'Fallon, Illinois was her second job as a counselor. She had spent the last several years at Twin Lakes High School in Monticello, Indiana before resigning and accepting her current position in O'Fallon as the Director of Guidance. It was a promotion and a welcomed change. Sometimes change was good for the soul. Even if the circumstances of her old life had left her broken-hearted.

Principal Sam Malone and Remi had kept their relationship confidential for several months before he got down on bended knee. They were in the school hallway bordered by lockers. It was late, and they were in the building alone. It wasn't the most romantic place he could have chosen to ask her to marry him, but that was Sam. Anything on his mind had to be expressed in the moment. It was one of the things Remi had loved about him. She didn't need flowers or dinner by candlelight. Only him.

But Sam needed more. And a newly hired, young school nurse had met his needs more than a few times before Remi discovered she was engaged to a man who was incapable of being faithful to her. And, of course — *he was sorry. It hadn't meant anything. It was only sex. Yes, more than once. He was stupid. He panicked about their commitment, but he was sure now. He wanted her. She had to forgive him.*

Remi didn't have to do anything. She was raised by parents who made senseless choices and expected for those indiscretions to be overlooked. No longer would she live her life in that way. Remi was done. She left her fiancé and her job. If she had learned anything from her beloved Sam, it was to act in the moment. While it was a rash decision to leave her life as she knew it behind, already Remi felt like she fit well into her new professional element. The high school students were primarily the same, and the staff were welcoming enough to her. The only thing that initially bothered her were the personal questions. *Are you married? Do you have children?* Remi kept to herself that she was reeling from a broken engagement. No one needed to know.

The most difficult part of her day was coming home to an empty house. She and Sam had been long accustomed to spending the night together. And once they were engaged,

Remi had moved in with him. When she left him and moved from Indiana to Illinois, she was unexpectedly homeless and chose to live in a hotel in the City of O'Fallon for several weeks until she found a new job and a home of her own. Accepting the guidance counselor position at a prominent high school in an altogether different state was a serious change in her life. And now she had chosen to become a recluse as a single woman again. *Work and home. Home and work.* That was Remi's life now. She didn't need or want anything more. She could take care of herself. While the pain of the breakup still chipped away at her heart, Remi realized she was more let down by not getting her happily ever after than she was with losing Sam. She was a guarded girl most of her life, considering her upbringing. Sam had broken through a wall in her heart, because she allowed him to. She had been in search of something more for herself than a life alone. But now, at thirty years old, she was back to believing that walling herself off from the world wasn't such a bad thing. She had her job, one that she loved. And she had a cozy new place to live. She didn't need anything more.

Remi tried not to stare as she walked around the back of her car in her open garage. Across the street, she saw activity on her neighbor's driveway. This time she saw the husband who lived there. He had a large white pickup truck and it was running loud, diesel loud. He killed the engine and stepped down from the truck. She stared and he immediately caught her eye. *How obvious. Ugh. He's looking back!* Remi awkwardly raised her hand and waved at him. Before he could wave back, she had already turned her body and walked further into the garage toward the door that led inside.

ooOO

Tucker stared back across the street. All he saw after that quick instant was the back of her head of long, dark, wavy hair. *Strange,* he thought. *Kate was right. The new neighbor was all to herself. Hardly a social butterfly. She never made an effort to introduce herself.* Those thoughts escaped him as soon as he turned to see Kate's SUV pulling onto the driveway.

He walked to her open window which she had lowered for him. He immediately peeked through it and into the backseat.

"Liv's still at after-school care. I told her I'd have her doll when I picked her up," Kate stated. There were toys that Livy left behind for when she stayed with her daddy, but she had missed one doll the night before and cried herself to sleep over it. Tucker would have rushed it over to her at any hour had he known. It wasn't until this morning when Kate texted that he was aware she wanted to pick up the doll.

Tucker looked disappointed. "I wanted to see her. I was looking forward to that all day." Tucker noticed the top three buttons were open on Kate's black shift dress. He hadn't remembered seeing that dress before. She looked beautiful to him, as always. Her makeup was still flawless, even after a full day of work.

"I'm sorry," Kate said, but she had not sounded sincere. "I didn't want to rush her visit. You'll see her tomorrow night, at this time."

Tucker nodded. He didn't want to argue with her. "How's she doing? Is she adjusting to her new home?"

Kate paused before she answered. "She's doing well. She misses you, but I know it will help when she's with you for a few days. We just need to get into a solid routine of passing her back and forth." That sounded harsh to Tucker, but it was a reality for them now.

"I miss her, too," he stated, feeling a pang of hurt rise to his chest. And the fact was, he missed his wife as well. She had so effortlessly moved on. He should resent her for that. But he didn't.

"Tucker, the doll. Can you go grab it?" Kate was obviously not going to move from the driver's seat of her Suburban, engine running.

"Seriously? Can't you come look for it? I'm not even sure which one it is..."

"It's the boy doll, the only boy she has. Powder blue sleeper. Pacifier in its mouth." Kate's description was precise enough. Tucker turned from the car window and sprinted up the driveway. It was understood that he would be right back.

It took him a few minutes to find the doll under a mound of others piled on top the pink toy box at the foot of Livy's toddler bed.

"That's the one," Kate said, taking it through the car window. "Thanks."

Tucker nodded. "Kiss Livy for me, and I'll Facetime her at seven tonight."

"We might be eating dinner then," Kate spoke with slight hesitation in her voice.

"At seven? Isn't that kind of close to her eight o'clock bedtime?" Tucker frowned. If there was anything he had learned from having a baby and later a toddler, it was the importance of a routine. *Mealtime. Bedtime.* Parents had to run a tight ship to keep little people on a healthy, balanced schedule.

"Riley works late, and we like to have dinner together…" *A different routine with a new family.* This moment was awkward between them now. Kate even had trouble spitting out those words without ceasing eye contact with him. And the thought of his daughter already having a replacement father in her life, for things like dinnertime, destroyed him. It tore him apart inside even more than the image of Kate in another man's bed. Riley whatever-the-hell-his-last-name-was was living *his life* with *his child* and soon to be ex-wife. The thought sickened Tucker, and he had to push it out of his mind every single time he went there.

Tucker only responded with a nod of his head. That was all this woman —who was about to no longer be his wife— deserved. He would play nice with her, for Livy's sake, but he did not have to pretend to like or care about Riley, the fucker who stole his family.

When Kate's vehicle rolled backward off the end of the driveway, Tucker stood there for a moment watching her leave. One day he knew he would be able to accept this change. But it wasn't going to be today.

Through the front window of her house, Remi stood watching what took place across the street. A baby doll was exchanged. They had a child. It should not have appeared odd. From her view, she had not even been able to see the blonde beauty Kate. Only the husband, whose name she did not know. His body language caught her attention. So much so that she had not been able to look away. He seemed forlorn. Sad or frustrated. His shoulders were slumped. He couldn't stand still, constantly moving one tapered leg of faded denim. And he repeatedly scuffed a brown work boot on the concrete. Was he suppressing anger or frustration? Remi was good at reading people's actions. It was part of her occupation. Something seemed off. But it was none of her business. She finally walked away from the window, and chided herself for teetering on the brink of allowing her lonely life to transform her into a nosy neighbor.

Chapter 3

Tucker fought a solemn feeling the moment he stepped inside his empty house after work. It was too quiet. He was alone. There was no plan for dinner and one person wasn't even worth cooking for. He wasn't hungry anyway. He thought about starting to go to the gym again in the evening, something he gave up doing regularly when Livy was born. He never could wait to get home to her, and once he was home he didn't want to leave her. Tucker was an attentive, affectionate father. Which was entirely the reason this adjustment without his family was sucking the life out of him.

He kicked off his work boots in the kitchen and made his way to the living room. He turned on the TV for background noise. He didn't care about the current events or the weather.

It never failed. He started thinking about what went wrong six months ago. His marriage had been solid, or so he had thought. Kate was high maintenance, but mostly everything about her made him smile. She was a girly girl. Clothes, shoes, makeup, a selective eater to maintain a slender figure. All of that and more he had accepted and loved about her. She was a paralegal for a law office in downtown St. Louis. She made serious money, in comparison to Tucker as the manager of a hardware store in O'Fallon. It used to not matter to Kate, or so she had said, that he didn't have a college education and a salary to match or surpass hers. And then she met Riley. A seasoned lawyer, nine years older than her. He was an upscale business man. Tucker was blue collar, and hard-working. He felt like less of a man after she eventually confessed that the weekly nights out with her girlfriends had really been a cover. She was having an affair. In a matter of six months, their marriage, their life as they knew it, was over. There wouldn't be a second child to complete their little family. Tucker no longer had a wife, a woman he was proud to call his partner. And his time with his child had spiraled into something called visitation and custody. He had absolutely no say-so in the destruction of his life. It was a sickening, hopeless feeling.

A loud sound of something, a bang that he immediately thought to be a crash outside of his house, forced Tucker out of his glum state. He ran to his front door and pulled it open. From there he saw a vehicle in the middle of the street. He recognized it to be the retired neighbor lady, Joy. She steered her minivan off the road, parked, and got out. By now, Tucker was making his way down his driveway in his white socks. He had not taken the time to stuff his feet back in his boots or grab another pair of shoes.

"Joy? You okay there?" Tucker called out to the white-haired woman in her sixties whom he had known for all of the five years he lived in that neighborhood with Kate.

Joy shook her head, bent down on the street, and picked up what looked to be her vehicle's passenger side mirror. "I got too close to the mailbox of our new neighbor." Joy looked emotional, as Tucker made his way across the street to her.

"Oh damn. That's not good. But it's just a mirror and mailbox. No real harm done." Tucker made his way around to the other side of her minivan, to assess the damage. He really wished he had his boots on. He felt like he was walking on nails, and as stiff and slow as an old man. The mailbox was ruined. It was a dated one anyway, he thought, but it was indeed smashed beyond repair. And the neighbor's mail was scattered on the ground. He bent down to retrieve the white envelopes and the scattered pages of a sale ad. He stood upright again next to Joy as she spoke nervously and fast. "I need to ring the doorbell and tell Remi. I hope she will understand. I'll pay for the damage, of course." Tucker nodded, and assumed *Remi* was their new neighbor's name. He obviously had been the last person to meet her, although he didn't think that Kate had gotten her name. If she had, she never said.

Tucker looked toward her house now, and saw their new neighbor walking down the driveway. "You'll have your chance to explain now," Tucker told Joy, as he stood stationary and readied to watch the exchange between them.

"Oh Remi, honey, I apologize for damaging your mailbox. How foolish of me! I had no idea I was so close to it." Joy held up her mirror as further explanation, and Tucker chuckled a little under his breath. It wasn't funny, but yet it was.

Remi's eyes widened. Tucker watched her closely. Her long dark hair was now pulled up into a messy, high bun. The color perfectly matched her dark eyes. She was wearing black yoga pants and a lime green tank top. Her after work clothes, he assumed. He was accustomed to seeing Kate do the same thing. Her body was different than Kate's. Kate strived to be thin, and had always been worried about gaining inches everywhere, but especially around her waistline. This woman embraced her curves. She wasn't plump, just shapely in all the right places. A handful of woman, a man would say. Tucker caught his eyes moving over her, and he stopped himself when he heard her speak for the first time. "Joy, right?" Joy nodded. "It's okay. It's completely fine," Remi sounded as if she was trying to reassure herself of that. Nonetheless she was trying to be compassionate, Tucker supposed. "I never liked the look of that box anyway and I'll be happy to replace it now." Remi laughed nervously after she spoke, in an attempt to ease Joy's embarrassment, but the older woman still looked sickened by the damage she had accidentally caused.

Tucker listened to their exchange. Joy would pay for a new mailbox. Remi said that wasn't necessary. But finally, she relented, and Joy was satisfied but had to rush off to pick up her grandchild from daycare. Remi assured her again that it was nothing to stress over. When Joy drove off, Tucker was still standing stocking footed near the curb at the base of what was left of the damaged mailbox.

"I'm Tucker Brandt," he said, as Remi turned to him. "We haven't officially met yet." She instantly admired how comfortable he appeared in his own skin. Remi focused on the mail she had already spotted in his hand.

"I'm Remi Jasper," she offered, and attempted a polite smile. This moment felt awkward. More unsettling than Joy being near tears over a mailbox and a detached, shattered passenger side mirror. Remi just wasn't as sure of herself anymore. Sam had robbed that from her. She no longer felt adequate around men. And the very last thing she wanted to do was get to know someone new. But she would be neighborly and friendly to this man who seemed genuine. He had a young family right across the street from her. Being cordial was the right thing to do.

"I have your mail," he spoke, reaching his hand to her. She took it from him. Her own hand was trembling.

"Thanks. Wow. I'm sorry, I guess I'm more frazzled than I thought," Remi admitted. "I heard the crash, but I was in the middle of changing clothes. I really didn't know what to expect when I came out here."

"It alarmed me, too. I hope Joy is alright, I mean to drive and all. I didn't want to make too big a deal of it, as I'm only a neighbor."

"Right. Well, you probably know her better than me. I just moved in."

"Yeah, I know. My wife, um," Tucker stopped himself. That was going to take some getting used to. "Kate said she met you."

"And your adorable little girl as well," Remi smiled, obviously sincerely, and Tucker did too. Conversation was easy when referring to children.

"Thank you." He missed Lizy terribly, but this wasn't the time or place or person to express it to.

Remi looked down at his feet. His socks. He noticed her staring.

"No time to grab shoes," he attempted to explain.

"I see that," she responded. "I hope you're not stepping in glass."

Tucker didn't think he was, but he did double-check the bottoms of both his feet anyway. "All clear, but I think I will get a broom to be sure you and I aren't backing out and driving through any broken glass on this road later."

"Or I could do that," Remi offered.

"I'll take care of it. Just need to get some shoes on first." He chuckled, and Remi nodded.

"Well thanks for my mail," Remi immediately cringed at what she said. *What a dumb thing to say.* She almost felt like a nervous school girl. And she chided herself for it. For what was running through her mind. His masculinity was sexy. Blue eyes. Short-cropped brown hair, much lighter brown than her own. His faded jeans form fitted his full thighs and rear end. Yes, she had noticed. *But he was a married man. A family man!* She willed herself not to blush.

Tucker began to walk away awkwardly in his socks on the rocks. "Not a problem. Welcome to the neighborhood. It's pretty quiet, except for when there are crashes." He winked, and Remi laughed a little.

"Not funny. Now I have to go new mailbox shopping." And install one, she thought, believing it couldn't be that difficult. *Could it?*

"I could help with that," he offered. "I manage a hardware store on State Street. Rix Hardware, if you know of it?"

"I may have to stop in there," she stated, and left it at that. Tucker turned around again to walk back across the street to retrieve a pair of shoes and a broom.

Chapter 4

Remi parked her compact Kia Sportage at an angle along the curb. She looked up at the sign that marked the building. *Rix hardware.* It looked like a ma and pa shop. Hardly a home improvement supplies and retail company like Lowes or Home Depot. That made her smile though. Those businesses were most definitely few and far between nowadays. This store was on her route, on her way home from the high school. She needed a mailbox as soon as possible. Those were both convenient reasons to stop there. And her neighbor suggested it. Before she stepped through the doorway of the store, she wondered if he would be working. She could use the guidance as she had never bought a mailbox before. She lived in an apartment in college and afterward, and when she moved into Sam's house, any home improvements were on his hands. Not that he was handy, he just knew how to hire out for odd jobs.

The glass door chimed above her head when she pulled it open and walked inside. The wood flooring was ancient, and worn. And there was a faint scent of bug spray in the store. A young kid behind the register awkwardly greeted her as she walked by. Remi smiled in return. The first aisle she walked down was the paint section. She thought about painting the living room walls in her house a bold color. White walls bored her and the entire house was full of them. Changing one room at a time was going to be her goal, eventually, but right now Remi was living on a budget. She had spent more money than she wanted to, living in the hotel for several weeks before she found and bought a house. She wasn't struggling financially, but she was trying to refrain from splurging on anything. If she painted, she would want to redecorate too. It was a chain reaction, so Remi reminded herself to just focus on finding a mailbox.

She walked up and down three different aisles and already wished she had initially asked the young man working the front register to point her in the right direction. She knew they stocked and sold mailboxes in that store. Her neighbor told her so.

"Against the back wall," Remi heard a male voice behind her. She turned around in the middle of the aisle.

He looked the same as he had that night on her curb when they swapped introductions. Tapered faded jeans. No visible white socks this time. He wore tan work boots. A charcoal grey polo shirt with Rix Hardware stenciled above his left breast. Remi momentarily felt overdressed in her work clothes. A straight black skirt that ended just above her knees and a beige blouse that hugged her waist and hips. She sometimes changed out of her heels to run errands after work, but right now her ballet flats took up space on the floor in the backseat of her Kia.

"Is it that obvious that I don't know my way around in here?" Remi asked, feeling her cheeks flush.

Tucker waved his hand in front of his face. "No one expects you to. I'm glad I spotted you. Let me show you what we have… to see if anything might be what you would like."

The aisle was wide enough for Tucker to walk beside her. He was only about an inch taller than her in heels. His biceps were thick near the elastic ends of his polo shirt. She wondered if he worked out at the gym. That was another thing she needed to get into the routine of doing again. Remi heard herself thank him and then they walked to the back of the store together. He was working. He was in his element, and obviously quite comfortable. He had no tags on him that told of his supervisor status there, but Remi thought she remembered Tucker saying that he was the manager.

"Straight from work, I guess?" he asked referring to her dress clothes, as they were almost to the very back wall, and he wondered if she would say what she did for a living. She was the quiet, reserved type. He guessed that about her already.

"Yes, right down the road, at the high school."

"So, you're a teacher?" Tucker asked, and Remi wasn't surprised. She often was on the receiving end of that assumption.

"Guidance counselor," she offered.

"Ah, wonderful. Kids need good listeners and sound advice nowadays. A lot goes on in their lives. So much more than I remember when I was that age."

Remi nodded. "Yes and no. The problems were present then too. Maybe just not as out there, front and center, as they are now with social media and a general lack of respect for people."

"Gotcha," Tucker nodded his head. She was a smart woman, he could tell. Or she just really knew her stuff in her element.

And now he was about to show her what he knew best. His merchandise. She stopped with him in front of the back wall. "Okay, so I'm not sure what you are wanting as a replacement for what you had. This kind was the original type that the Zurliene's had before you moved in to their former house." He tapped two of his fingers on a black galvanized steel construction mailbox. Remi saw the price tag was $34.95. She was prepared to just decide on that one, but then Tucker spoke again. "Or, we have the more modernized keystone look, where the box itself is black, but the lid and flag are bronze. A little fancier and sturdier look, if you're interested in that." Remi saw the price of that one was considerably more at $168.97.

"To be honest, I came in here thinking I would buy cheap," Remi let out a nervous laugh, and Tucker chuckled and nodded. "But I could see that one at the end of my driveway." The landscape on the ground around the mailbox had a rose bush and large white stone rock. A plain old mailbox didn't belong there anymore, Remi thought, but the high price of a fancier one was not something she intended to spend.

"I understand both ways. I've worked in small town retail for more than a dozen years now, and that's one complaint I do have. We aren't a giant chain store with a wide selection. For the mailboxes it's cheap or expensive. The manager before me used to push the more expensive things in here and he would say go big, or go home. I am not that way.

And I will not be offended if you walk out of here and choose to look elsewhere for a better deal."

Remi stared at him longer than she wanted to before she glanced at both of her choices to purchase. She could wait on that gym membership and just take up running down the street, or on the old treadmill in her basement – as that was free. "I think I'll go big and go home."

Tucker paused before he laughed. Remi was smiling at him. "The fancy one?"

Remi nodded. "Yeah… I'll take it." Spending almost two hundred dollars on a mailbox felt crazy to her, but on impulse she wanted something better than what she had.

"Alright then," Tucker grabbed one of its exact kind in a sealed box from a higher shelf. "Your wooden post is still in good condition on the existing one, so this is all you will need." He wondered if she had someone… a father, a brother… a boyfriend… to install it for her. But he didn't believe it was appropriate to ask.

"Okay good, thank you, I didn't even think about that." Remi paused. She wanted to ask him if they offered any services there to help with home installation. She still didn't trust herself to know what she was doing, but imagined it could not be too difficult to screw a box on a pole.

"If that's all, you can check out up front, if you want to walk with me," Tucker offered.

"That's all," she nodded, and they moved in unison to the front of the store. Tucker wasn't one to share silence in a comfortable way, especially in his work environment. So, he spoke again.

"I don't want to speculate how handy you are or if you have someone in mind to put this baby on the post," Tucker shook the box in his hands, "but I am capable if you need to give someone a holler."

Remi laughed. It was as if he was reading her mind. She didn't, however, want him to think of her as helpless or needy. Yes, she was a woman living on her own, but she didn't need a man. Not anymore. "I think I can handle it, but thank you for offering."

"Absolutely," Tucker nodded. And once they reached the single check-out desk in the front of the store, Tucker placed the box on the conveyer belt and the young man working the register seemed just as tense as he had appeared to be earlier. "How ya doin', Bobby?" Tucker asked him. "It's Bobby's first week with us and he's handling things like a boss." Remi smiled. *Her neighbor truly was a nice guy.*

"I'd like you to meet the delivery truck around back and direct them where to unload the ceiling fans." Tucker looked at Bobby and he in turn accepted the order. When he walked away, Tucker stepped behind the cash register to help Remi. Remi reached for her handbag on her shoulder. She was no longer going to spend the cash in her wallet to pay for the replacement mailbox. She would use her credit card for this purchase.

"I want to be clear that I didn't splurge on this mailbox because Joy insisted on paying for it. In fact, I'm not charging her this full amount." Tucker smiled. He had actually forgotten about Joy's insistence to cover the cost for the replacement mailbox. Remi's words spoke volumes. *She had a kind heart.*

"I honestly did not think that at all," Tucker told her. "You do what's best for yourself. Joy can handle a splurge. She lives well in retirement, and besides I know she felt awful about the little accident."

Remi smiled. "It's fine. It could have been much worse. No one got hurt."

"That's for sure. No kids on the road, thank goodness." Tucker thought of Livy. He could hardly wait to go home after work, and for Kate to drop her off. He wanted to pick her up at her new house, but Kate obviously had not been ready for that yet as she had brushed off his offer.

"How old is your little girl?" Remi asked, since he had mentioned kids in their neighborhood.

"She's three," he beamed, and she noticed.

"So little yet," Remi stated.

"Yeah, but she's grown fast. She has the vocabulary and comprehension skills of a five-year-old." It saddened Tucker to know that he was missing more growth and so many little moments in her life now that they were all no longer together as a family. Remi noticed the change in his demeanor, but he recovered quickly as he scanned the barcode on the box. She watched him punch a few codes on the computer keyboard before he turned to her with the total of her purchase. "With the new customer discount, your total is one-fifty even."

Remi's eyes widened. "That's considerably less than the regular price. Is there really such a thing as a new customer discount?"

"If you know me, there is. Please accept it. Consider it a housewarming gift for my new neighbor since I'm not into making casseroles or picking out a nice candle centerpiece."

Remi giggled, and felt heat on her cheeks again. "It's too much, but so kind of you. Thank you."

"Good. You're welcome," Tucker offered to carry the somewhat heavy box out to her vehicle, but Remi declined, and told him that she could manage. She sincerely thanked him again and Tucker, in turn, expressed his appreciation to her for doing business there. He smiled when he watched her for a moment through the window as she walked to her vehicle parked at an angle on the curb. And then he opened his wallet and counted out the cash to add to the register drawer. It was his gift to her, not a substantial discount from Rix Hardware.

Chapter 5

After Remi's sale, Tucker left the hardware store for the day. In less than an hour, he had to be home and ready for Livy. She was going to stay with him for two nights. It had only been a few days since his wife and little girl left, but to Tucker it felt like an eternity. FaceTime every evening wasn't enough. He wanted to hold his little girl in his arms. Act silly. Laugh. Play. He had all her favorite foods, and he planned to take her on a long bike ride to the park. It was going to strictly be their time together now, and he wanted to make memories with her. It wasn't difficult to entertain a three-year-old, and Livy was an easy, fun-loving child anyway. Tucker relished being a father, and he wished for more children – even as unlikely as that seemed right now.

He drove his truck down the street of the cul-de-sac where he lived, and before he turned onto his driveway he noticed Remi was home. Her garage door was open, her vehicle was pulled in. He glanced at the post, sans a mailbox, at the curb. He wondered if someone would stop by her house to help her. He was curious about her, or maybe he just sympathized with her because she too lived alone. For all he knew, she may have preferred her life that way. He, however, was having a difficult time adjusting to being alone. He imagined having Livy with him for a couple of days would rejuvenate him. Until she had to leave again.

He stepped down from his truck on the driveway. It was too immense to fit into the garage, and he was used to parking outside as they had a one-car garage and Kate's SUV had managed to fit snugly into it. He turned his head now and saw Kate arriving already. They were early, and he was instantly ready. All he wanted to do was see his little girl. He opened the backseat door behind Kate's driver seat the moment she shifted into park. "We're early," he heard Kate say, and she began to offer an explanation why, but Tucker never heard the rest. He didn't pay attention to anything else once he saw the excitement on Livy's face as she blurted out, "daddy!" Tucker unbuckled her seatbelt quickly and she threw herself into his arms. Kate stepped down onto the concrete and he saw the sincere smile on her face as she watched them together. She was holding a backpack and a couple of baby dolls, and she allowed the two of them a moment to reconnect.

"I want to see my room!" Livy exclaimed, as Tucker held her close.

"Well good, but we have a lot of playing to do before it's sleepy time." Tucker laughed when his little girl squealed.

"Do you want to come inside?" Tucker asked Kate, as she stood there still holding all of Livy's things. He would have taken them from her, but he had his arms full of his little love.

Kate shook her head. "I can't stay," she immediately spoke. "That's why we are early. I'm meeting Riley back in St. Louis for dinner on The Hill."

Tucker wanted to roll his eyes. Their schedules entirely revolved around *Riley*. He didn't want to waste his time talking or thinking about that guy. He had noticed that Kate was dressed to the nines again. This time she was wearing a red sleeveless jumper that form-fitted her chest and torso and was wide legged. Her matching heels were at least three-inches high. *She was such a glam girl.* And he knew her well. All of those dinner dates weren't about the food for her. He would even bet she consumed very little of it. For her, it was about the big city atmosphere, getting dolled up, and feeling prestigious.

"Okay," Tucker nodded, and shifted Livy in his arms so he could reach for her things. He wanted to say, *we will see you in a few days*, and brush Kate off as he felt like she had done to him when she took their daughter to live somewhere else, but he was more sympathetic than that. He didn't want to hurt her. He waited while Kate stepped closer to Livy in his arms. He could smell her familiar perfume, and her arm brushed his while she reached for their daughter.

"Be good for daddy, okay baby girl? I love you so much." Kate kissed her quickly on the lips, and Tucker held his breath being that close to her again. He had not been able to just shut off his feelings for her, like she obviously had for him.

"You stay too, mommy…" Livy spoke and sounded as if she was near tears.

"Oh honey, I can't. I don't live here anymore. But you are so lucky, you get to live in two houses!" Livy's face lit up to mimic her mother's excitement.

Yeah…we're all so lucky, Tucker thought and inhaled a slow, deep breath.

"Call me if you need me!" Kate made direct eye contact with Tucker, and a few seconds later, she was gone.

She wasn't a people watcher. She didn't spy out of windows. She could not have cared less what other people did with their lives. Unless it was one of the students at school who needed direction. But the activity across the street had grabbed her attention again. She had not seen that little family just exist together in that house, or yard. It seemed as if Kate and the child were always coming or going – and only Tucker was around. The actual exchange of Livy and a little backpack peaked Remi's interest today. But when she realized her things were likely packed for a daycare or preschool, it didn't seem so strange anymore. Remi did notice while they were both very affectionate with their little girl, they were not with each other. It was none of her concern. *"Mind your own business, Remi,"* she uttered aloud to herself. *"You've got a mailbox to install."*

∞∞

Livy only ate two forkfuls of macaroni and cheese. Tucker offered to make her a hot dog but she told him that her mommy does not let her eat those anymore. He never pushed the issue, or forced her to eat anything else at dinnertime. They ended up going outside to play. Tucker didn't stress over how much his child ate, or what she ate. She would eat something when she was hungry. It used to drive Kate to the brink when he would say that. He pushed that thought from his mind. He was a single dad now. Sure, he and Kate were co-parents, but when Livy was with him, it was his sole right to take care of her in his own way now.

On the front lawn, there was a doll stroller with no baby doll in it, a wiffle ball and bat, and a miniature plastic watering can with a single dandelion currently stuck inside it, mimicking a flower and vase. Those were the things that Livy hauled out of the garage and randomly played with while Tucker was on the driveway hooking up the bike trailer to his all-terrain bicycle. He had already promised Livy a ride to the park. From his squatted position on the driveway, he noticed Remi in her garage across the street. She was opening the box with her new mailbox in it. This he had to see. He wondered if she was going to install it herself. He wasn't by any means mocking her, or women in general. He wasn't sexist. Many women could do handywork. His wife never could, nor had she ever attempted to. He was used to hearing, *honey do this for me, so I don't break a nail, or get sweaty.* Yes, Kate was high maintenance. And he could already tell the woman across the street was not at all like her.

Remi saw her neighbors outside. She contemplated waiting for them to leave on what looked like was going to be a bike ride in a matter of minutes. She made the mistake of glancing across the street from inside of her garage when Tucker caught her eye.

"You okay with that over there?" Tucker called out to her. He thought about respecting the boundaries, between two people who were practically strangers, because he had already offered his help. But something forced him to just go for it.

"I think so," Remi called back, "except for the fact that I just read in the instructions that I need a power drill." She frowned. *Had she really thought a screwdriver would be all she needed?* She didn't want to admit it, but she needed help.

"Wait one second," she heard him holler back in response. Remi then watched him round up his little girl from the front yard as they both made their way into their own garage. A moment later, Tucker carried a cordless power drill in one hand and his daughter in the crick of his other arm, while he walked across the street. She met them at the curb, with her new mailbox in the open cardboard box.

"Hi," Remi said, feeling embarrassed to accept his help, but she quickly focused her eyes on his little blonde-haired girl. "How are you today, Livy?"

Livy smiled. She wasn't shy with strangers. "Daddy is going to take me for a bike ride."

"That sounds like so much fun," Remi responded to the child, and immediately felt guilty for delaying their fun. "The mailbox can wait," she told Tucker.

"Nonsense. There's time for both. This will only take a little while." Tucker set Livy down on her feet on the driveway. For a moment, Remi wondered how he was going to entertain her while he worked. But then she had her answer.

"I'll help you, daddy." Remi smiled at the two of them together. He had such patience with her. She heard him tell her to hold out her hand. In her tiny open palm, he placed one of the brackets from inside of the box. He told her what it was called and how it was going to help secure the mailbox on that wooden post. Livy listened intently. She was clearly grown up for three years old.

While Tucker emptied the contents of the box —more of the brackets and the actual mailbox— Livy kept talking. The little one's next comment forced Tucker to stop working for a moment when Livy had looked Remi directly in the eye and said, *"my mommy and daddy don't live in the same house anymore."*

Remi was sure she had heard her right, and before she could opt to ignore the comment and change the subject, Tucker stood tall on his feet. He tousled the blonde hair on Livy's head before he spoke. "Kate and I are getting a divorce." He looked pained to speak those words, and Remi suddenly felt saddened for him and his little girl.

"Daddy lives there," Livy pointed across the street, "and I live with mommy and Riley. But I'm home with my daddy for two nights."

Remi nodded her head. Such a complicated life for a little one to understand. At this point, Remi wanted to understand more. *What went wrong in their marriage? And who was Riley?* She had an obvious hunch that the two were correlated.

She wanted to say she was sorry that he was dealing with the end of his marriage, but she couldn't speak of it in front of a child, nor did she think it would be appropriate to assume that Tucker didn't want the divorce. This was a private, personal matter, and Remi just needed to keep herself out of it.

"That's right," Tucker spoke to Livy, "now let's get back to work so Remi can have a new mailbox ready, otherwise the mailman will not know where to put her mail if she only has a bare post stuck in the ground." Livy giggled, and Remi was relieved to have the awkward subject of failed relationships dropped.

Chapter 6

Livy stayed close to her daddy the entire time he installed the mailbox. Remi stood near them as well. She watched how Tucker seemed to have everything handled. Effortlessly. They shared small talk while he worked, and Livy was the center of most of it.

"All set," Tucker said, taking a step back, off the curb, to get a better look at his handywork.

"It looks great, thank you," Remi said. "What do I owe you for this?"

Tucker waved a hand in front of his face. "Absolutely nothing. I'm happy to help. You bought it from Rix, that's thanks enough."

"I appreciate that," Remi said, but she still felt a little bit indebted to him. Like maybe she should cook and deliver dinner to him, or purchase a gift card for him and Livy to dine out somewhere. She caught herself feeling sad for him. He no longer had a wife. As far as she knew, Tucker was probably more self-sufficient than most men. Even still, Remi wanted to do something nice for him to show her gratitude sometime soon.

"Can we go on a bike ride now?" Livy tugged on Tucker's jeans at the knee. He had knelt on the lawn while he worked, and both of his faded knees were grass stained.

"We sure can. Let me put up my drill." As Tucker squatted to pick up the trash and place it into the empty box, Remi bent forward. "I'll take care of it. You go take that bike ride." A plastic baggie that held the bolts was on the ground by Tucker's boot, and when Remi reached for it, their hands brushed against each other. They simultaneously pulled away. Tucker saw Remi's cheeks flush, as she continued to look down at the ground. He let her take the plastic bag. Her eyes were the darkest shade of brown, he noticed again, as she had made fleeting eye contact with him just now.

"Okay then," Tucker started to walk back across the street, directly behind Livy. "Let's hope Joy steers clear of your new mailbox. Literally."

Remi laughed out loud. "Let's hope!" She was surprised at how comfortable she felt with him – with both of them. Remi watched the two walk away. She was grateful for her new neighbors. They were caring people, sans Kate in her opinion. *What kind of woman left a man like Tucker?*

ထထ

A couple days passed since Remi had any interaction with Tucker and his little girl. She did see them, from her window, coming or going or just playing in the front yard. But she hadn't stopped to watch them as she was right now. This time she knew what was happening when Kate's full-size black SUV rolled up onto the driveway and sat idle. Kate no longer lived in that house, nor did Livy full-time. The thought of their young family, just barely beginning their lives together, now being broken, saddened Remi.

Livy was dragging her backpack on the ground, and Remi watched Tucker take it from her and then he swung it over his broad shoulder. By now Kate had stepped down from her vehicle. After the door opened, Remi saw her straw-colored wedges on the concrete first. It was Saturday and she obviously was not one who liked to dress down.

Livy ran to Kate, and Kate bent her knees to catch her little girl in her arms. When she stood back up to her full height, with Livy on her hip, Tucker was standing directly in front of her. His eyes looked sad. Two nights had gone too fast. And this was the first time he truly felt what joint custody meant. There were now going to be a lot of happy and excited hellos, as well as sad goodbyes. His time with Livy was extra special now. He had to hold onto that truth, and stay positive. He couldn't dwell on how sad he felt knowing the house was going to be quiet and he would be alone again for another few days.

"Did you have a good time with daddy?" Kate asked, kissing her daughter on one cheek multiple times.

"Uh huh," Livy nodded, amidst giggles, and looked back at Tucker. He winked at her in return.

"Well, thank daddy for a fun time, and tell him you will see him again in just a few days." Kate handed Livy over to Tucker for the goodbye she initiated. She uttered, *thanks daddy,* as he held her close and kissed the top of her blonde head.

"No thanks necessary, baby girl. I will talk to you soon, okay?" Tucker moved to place Livy inside of her car seat after he noticed Kate had already opened the backseat door. She was in a hurry to get going. She was always in a rush to leave now. She had another life to get back to. *Riley was waiting.*

Once Tucker said his final goodbyes to Livy, he closed the door to the backseat. Kate hadn't gotten back into the driver's seat, and Tucker noticed a paper-clipped stack of papers in her hand that she had not been holding earlier.

He looked down at that, and then back up at her. She looked uncomfortable. Tucker had known Kate long enough to recognize her emotions. "Take these," she spoke. "Read them over, and sign. I'd like to have them back next time Livy's with you."

Tucker reached for the papers, and his eyes focused on the bold print at the top of the page. DIVORCE AGREEMENT.

"You're all set, huh?" he asked her, trying to disguise the emotion in his own voice. He knew she had already filed the motion to end their marriage, and he assumed her live-in lover, and lawyer, was taking care of the proceedings. Tucker just didn't think it would come together so soon.

"I am. I mean, we are," Kate sounded nervous, but she kept full-on eye contact with Tucker. She looked serious. And, of course, he already knew all too well that she was dead serious about ending their marriage. "It's all there, everything we agreed on. Joint custody. No child support from either of us, because we are equally sharing our time raising her." Kate didn't want anything that Tucker had, certainly not his money because he didn't have any. His paycheck never did match hers.

Tucker rolled the papers in his hands until he was holding them in the shape of a narrow cylinder. "Okay," he responded, and that was all. Kate knew better than to expect anything more from him. He couldn't fight this. Even if he wanted to. Their marriage was over because Kate wanted it to be. Their family was wrecked because she wanted out. Her heart wasn't in it anymore. But they both wholeheartedly agreed to still be the best parents possible for Livy. Tucker forced himself to focus on that now. He stepped back from Kate, and even though he could not see her through the tinted window, Tucker called out. "I love you, Livs. See you soon." And then he heard her sweet little voice say, "Bye daddy."

∞∞

Remi wasn't entirely sure what had taken place, but she had a hunch. She stepped out the front door of her house as the SUV drove off, down the road of their private cul-de-sac with only one outlet. Her hair was up in a messy bun, and she wore no makeup. Leggings and an oversized t-shirt were all she had managed to throw on. She was grateful she had a bra on too as she practically marched down her driveway in bare feet, without rethinking her appearance. *What did she think she was going to say to him? What was her excuse right now?* Remi clearly had not thought about how obvious she was being.

Tucker was still on the driveway when Remi called out to him. "Hey, um, I couldn't help but notice that Livy left with her mom. You okay?" She surprised herself with her own words. She didn't reach out to people in her personal life. Not anymore. She chose to cut herself off from the world. *Work, home. Home, work. Remember?* She was having a war of words inside of her own head as she reached the curb at the end of her driveway. She was barefoot, so she stopped before stepping onto the street.

Tucker walked on the rocks toward her. He was wearing his standard look of jeans and a t-shirt, this one was plain white. He wore gray tennis shoes instead of work boots, she noticed. "I'm fine, thanks. It's something I'll just have to get used to."

Remi nodded. She wondered if she overstepped. "Livy adores you."

Tucker smiled wide. "Yeah, the feeling is mutual." Tucker stopped when he met her at the curb across the street from his house. He held up the papers, still in the shape of that cylinder, now in just one hand. "Kate left me with some reading material." Remi listened raptly, without saying a word in response. "Sign on the dotted line, well it's probably not dotted," he let out a nervous chuckle, "and my marriage is officially over. I'll have an ex-wife. It doesn't seem real, you know?"

Remi spoke sincerely. Again, she didn't know what she was doing. A part of her wished she had just stayed safely inside of her home. *Look. Watch. But don't let yourself be seen or forced to interact.* She felt compelled to be out there. To be there for him. Tucker was a good man, as far as she could tell. And Remi believed she was a decent judge of character. *She had misread her own fiancé though…*

"I'm sorry that she hurt you," were the first words out of her mouth. Remi most definitely understood pain inflicted by others. "People can be so careless with each other's hearts." It was obvious to Tucker that Remi saw him as the one left behind, rather than the one who wanted the divorce.

"Me, too. Thank you. She left me for another man. I may as well just get that out in the open. She and my daughter live with him now. He's a bigshot lawyer in St. Louis. I'm just a handyman who manages a ma and pa shop in a much smaller city."

"Don't," Remi spoke immediately. "Be kind to yourself. None of us should compare ourselves with anyone. Our focus should be on being the best version of ourselves."

Tucker smiled. "This is the first time I've heard the counselor talk come out of you."

Remi laughed a little. "She emerges from time to time." So much of what Remi said was easier spoken than truly and personally lived out. She was just as guilty as anyone when she, actually just moments ago, compared herself to Kate. *Kate was a beautiful blonde. Remi was an attractive brunette. She had a few nice features.* She believed that about herself. *Kate was thin. Remi was thicker. She wasn't overweight. She had curves. She had muscle. But she was far from model status,* she again believed.

"Good advice," Tucker nodded. "I am proud of what I have. I am," he said, as if he was trying to convince himself. "It's just my ego has taken a blow. When a woman you pledge your life to, who has lived with you and been right by your side for almost a half a dozen years, chooses better," he paused, "well, you can't help but feel bruised. She's living in a bigger, fancier, newer house with a man who makes a ridiculous amount of money."

"Bruises heal," Remi stated in reference to his ego. "They hurt, and sometimes they run really deep. They might turn a cluster of ugly colors before they completely disappear, but one day you will never be able to tell that there was pain."

"Are you speaking from experience?" Tucker asked her, giving her a dose of how personal she had been with him since she walked down her driveway in leggings that didn't conceal the sexy curves on the lower half of her body.

"Time will tell," she winked. And then, for some reason, she decided to say more. "Whether I want to admit it or not, my bruises are still in the ugly stage." Tucker wondered where her pain had stemmed from. *Who, or what, had made those beautiful, deep brown eyes cry?* But he didn't want to push, as this was the first time since he met Remi that she had not appeared entirely closed off.

Tucker stood there, and he only looked at her for a long, silent, moment. Shared pain between two people sometimes formed a bond, or a friendship. He liked how he felt right now. *Like someone else understood.* She wasn't his mother trying to make it all better with words like *give it time, keep yourself busy.* She wasn't his brother who had been married for the last decade and hopefully would never feel the pain of having the love of his life tell him *she's done. She's leaving. She had fallen for someone else.* She wasn't his guy friends who rallied for him, and then told him how lucky he was to be unattached. *Get drunk. Get laid.* His brother had said as much, too.

No, Remi wasn't like all the others. He spoke this time when he looked at her. "This may be crazy, but would you like to have lunch, or dinner? I don't know what's on your schedule. I just know that talking to you like this has made me forget all about how much I hate to see my child leave again for awhile."

"I'm happy I could help a little," Remi responded, quickly searching her mind, her immediate somewhat frantic thoughts, for an excuse to tell Tucker *no, she was not interested.* But instead, she heard herself reply, "How about dinner later?"

Chapter 7

Remi stood in front of the closet in her bedroom. The mirrored door was wide open, and she wore only her black bra and matching panties. She had taken a shower and blow dried her hair, which fell onto her shoulders in loose curls. Her hair was naturally curly when she didn't try to tame it with a flat iron or product. She applied her makeup with more care than usual. She never went anywhere else except for work and running errands. She didn't need to look the part for anyone. But tonight was different. She liked Tucker. She wanted him to see her as pretty. She was hardly Kate-like, which was an appearance of perfection, Remi believed, but Tucker had obviously liked something about her or he would not have asked her out. If anything, Remi enjoyed talking to him. He didn't have to know that she had a slight crush on him. If he needed someone to talk to, to see him through this rough time in his life, Remi could be that person for him. Tucker had taken her mind off how messed up her own life had become. They found a connection already. Even if it was merely about loneliness, it was still worth agreeing to a dinner date.

Remi had no idea where they were going. Tucker only said he would pick her up a few minutes before six o'clock. Remi wished now that she had his cell phone number, so she could send him a quick text. *What to wear? Are we going some place casual or dressy?* While she guessed Tucker was not the dress-up type, Remi chose a black shift dress with cap sleeves and a ruffled hem that she had not worn in awhile. She slipped into a pair of black wedges. When she left her bedroom, she sized herself up in the full-length closet door mirror. And she felt pretty. It had been a long time since she thought that way about herself. A two-timing fiancé had stolen that from her.

Ten minutes before six o'clock, Remi heard the diesel engine of Tucker's truck across the street. And through her front window, she watched him back out of his driveway and directly onto hers. She smiled at that. It was kind of silly, but she was amused anyway. She stepped out of her front door just as Tucker was getting out of his truck.

He looked at her for a moment. She hoped he thought she looked nice. "I was going to be a gentleman and knock..."

Remi met him on the sidewalk after she closed and locked her front door. "I'm sure you were. I didn't want to keep you waiting." She looked at him, long. He was wearing dark-washed jeans, and a long-sleeve white oxford shirt. He wore pointed-toe charcoal gray cowboy boots that made him at least two inches taller than her in wedges.

"I hope I'm dressed okay," he said, still looking at her. All of her. "I'm a denim kind of guy."

She laughed. "You look great. I'm not really all that dressy. A girl can wear a little black dress anywhere, right?"

Tucker let out a deep chuckle, but quickly turned serious. "You look beautiful." *Beautiful? He thought she looked beautiful?*

She felt cute. Okay, she felt pretty. But beautiful? Remi's cheeks flushed as she responded, "thank you."

Tucker followed Remi around to the passenger side of his truck. He opened the door for her. *A gentleman.* Remi was careful to use the running boards on the truck to boost herself up. In a somewhat short dress, she did her best to be ladylike. She looked at Tucker once she was seated. He smiled at her from where he stood outside the open door before he stepped back, closed her door, and walked around the front of the truck.

Remi inhaled a deep breath before he was seated beside her. She was nervous. "Where are we going for dinner?" she asked him as he shifted the truck into drive and gently rolled forward off the curb at the end of her driveway.

"What do you like? McDonalds? Taco Bell? Chick Fil A?"

Remi's eyes widened. "Okay, I may be a tad overdressed for Ronald McDonald."

Tucker laughed out loud. "Is there any type of food that you do not like? Could you go for a juicy steak?"

Remi's face already ached from smiling at him. He was a country boy to her. So unlike Sam. Or any man she had ever dated. He was down-to-earth and kind-hearted to the core. "That sounds delicious."

Their dinner and conversation at Andria's Steakhouse on Old Collinsville Road in O'Fallon were beyond Remi's expectations. It was, of course, her first time there. The restaurant was a chophouse, noted for serving steaks with a signature brush-on sauce. It was a supper-club setting, and Remi felt at ease in a dress and on Tucker's arm. She never once thought about who they might bump into there. *Someone from school? A neighbor they shared?* It never mattered to her the entire evening.

As they drove away from the restaurant, Tucker turned to her. "You know an awful lot about me. I appreciate your listening ear tonight. But, it's your turn now. I know the professional side to you. I like hearing about Remi the counselor, I do. I'd also like to know about you, personally."

Remi knew this was coming, but what did it matter? She could share her story with him, as he had done so openly, and no holds barred, with her.

She began with telling him that her father abandoned her after her parents divorced. And she admitted that her mother was never a woman to look up to, and their relationship became, and remained, strained once Remi reached adulthood.

"No parents you can count on? What about siblings?" Tucker asked as they drove home in the dark.

"None. It's just me."

"Have you ever been married?" That wasn't a strange question for Tucker to ask now that he was going through a divorce. And it wasn't so odd for Remi to hear, considering she was already thirty years old. From their earlier conversation, she gathered that Tucker was thirty-six.

"Close. Engaged for five months. Two months shy of the wedding when my fiancé cheated on me with the school nurse."

"Ouch. I'm sorry. I can honestly say I've been there. Well, not with the school nurse!" Tucker quickly corrected himself and they both laughed.

"I left. I left him so fast that I ended up jobless and homeless. A move to a different state, a hotel for several months, O'Fallon Township High School, and the house directly across the street from yours have put me on a new, hopefully better, path."

Tucker smiled. "Hopefully. I'm sorry to hear about your fiancé. I guess it's better to have happened before you were married, or before you had kids. No," Tucker quickly retracted his comment. He was speaking from experience, but having Livy was one thing he would never regret. "I don't mean that at all. I love my daughter, and even though divorcing Kate is the absolute hardest thing I've ever been through —and so much of my pain involves Livy— I need her. She's my whole life now."

Remi swallowed the lump that had suddenly formed deep in her throat. To have a father love her that way was always her greatest wish as a child. Livy was one lucky little girl. And Kate was a fool. Remi believed that now more than ever. "I understand," was all Remi could muster the words to say.

"Do you want children of your own?" Tucker asked, as they neared their subdivision on the north end of the City of O'Fallon. Their separate homes were near Estelle Kampmeyer Elementary School, which was where both Tucker and Kate had agreed they wanted Livy to attend. The school system in O'Fallon was top-notch. Remi understood that. The reputation of that district, from grade school to high school, was what prompted her on impulse to make the move there.

Remi paused before she answered. "I've never said no when I've been asked that question," she began, "but I have doubted my answer in my mind. My own mother was not at all good at being a parent. What if I inherited that from her?"

Tucker shook his head. "Good parenting coincides with having a good heart. You reach out to children every single day in your job. They may be young adults with big issues on their shoulders, or raging hormones, but they are still kids in so many other ways – and it sounds as if you have quite a way with them."

"Thank you," Remi spoke sincerely. She had never thought of her job and her possible role as a mother one day being correlated.

Tucker drove onto her driveway and he killed the engine. Remi hesitated for a moment before she spoke to him. "Would you like to come inside for a drink before your long drive home?"

They laughed in unison. "If it's okay with you, yes." Remi never would have offered if it was not *okay* with her.

∞∞

She gave him a beer, because that's what he drank at the restaurant. He had ordered one beer and she had a single glass of wine. She wondered after their dinner if he wanted another drink as she had then. And still now. The alcohol calmed her nerves, but it had not clouded her judgement. She enjoyed being with Tucker. The conversation never stopped, and it had been interesting and meaningful for her. Not just filler to pass the time, or to ward off awkward silence.

They sat down on her living room sofa, which was off-white suede. Remi kicked off her wedges and Tucker smiled inside. She felt at home. Not just because she was physically at her home, but with him there she had felt comfortable. Her toes were painted fire red, and he felt himself tighten between his legs. When he first met her, he thought of her as reserved or somewhat introverted. As he was getting to know her, he saw her as almost the complete opposite. There was a fiery side to her. He was attracted to her, but startled at the thought of being with someone new. After several years with Kate, he knew what she wanted and how she preferred to be touched and held. Tucker didn't know what to think about the idea of starting over with another woman. He pushed that thought from his mind. He enjoyed Remi's company. Nothing more was expected of him, or her, tonight. He certainly didn't want to overstep and scare her off. They were neighbors, after all. Friends too, he hoped.

"I want to paint in here," she spoke, referring to the living room. "I need more color in my life. These walls all throughout this house are so boring as plain white."

Tucker nodded. "Women like a little color. By far, more women than men buy paint from me at the shop."

"That's interesting," she noted.

"Yeah, it is. So what color in here?"

"Something dark, like maroon maybe?"

"Oh wow, that would be a change for sure."

"Good or bad?" she asked him with a smirk.

"Neither. If it's what you like, just make it your own." Tucker had a way with words which made Remi feel as if her opinion mattered.

"I think I will. And you will have to come back to see the changes."

Tucker clanked his glass beer bottle with her wine glass, and then they both at once took sips of their alcohol.

"I want you to know something," Tucker began, and Remi turned further into him on the sofa. "This was a date tonight. I had not planned it. It just came about. And I'm glad that it did."

"Me too," Remi agreed, wondering if he was going to kiss her soon. He still held his beer in his hand, so she kept her stemless wine glass close too. She took another long sip as he continued.

"I am not looking for a woman to replace the one I just lost," he admitted. "I actually thought I would be alone for a long time. I am just not the kind of guy who gets drunk and sets out to get laid."

Remi bit her bottom lip. *Was he for real? Or was this some sort of seduction line?*

"But I enjoy talking to you, and being with you like this," he admitted. "It's just one of those things that I already feel like it has fallen into my lap. I know we are both hurting from a broken relationship, but tonight, spending time with you, it just doesn't feel as raw."

"I know what you mean," Remi agreed. She most definitely had felt all the things he described.

"Should I get going while I'm still in your good graces?" he asked. "What I mean is, I'm attracted to you, but I don't want to end this date doing anything you or I aren't yet comfortable with."

Remi took ahold of his beer bottle and then set both it and her wine glass down on the sofa table in front of them. Tucker watched her with curious eyes.

"Tucker?" she spoke his name in question.

"Yes?"

"Do you always talk so much?"

He laughed, and he placed his open palm on the side of her cheek. She flushed. He moved closer. Their lips met. And their worlds collided. It was new. It was different. And their physical chemistry was overpowering.

She opened her mouth and his kiss deepened. Their bodies moved closer together. She was pressing her breasts to his chest. Through their clothing, there was an undeniable heat.

She ran her hands through his short-cropped hair. He gently brushed back her long, dark locks to bare her neck. She arched her back when his lips met the base of her neck. She couldn't get enough of his lips. *Lordy, this man liked to kiss.* His hands trailed down her back and around her waist to the top of her thigh. Her dress had been raised high on her leg with all the movement between them. He moved his hand underneath it and between her legs. All the while they were kissing with a shared mounting passion. Remi undid the buttons on his shirt and smoothed both of her palms on his bare chest. He groaned a little. "It's been a really long time," he admitted, and Remi imagined Kate rejecting his advances while she was having a sordid affair with another man. She needed to stop thinking about Kate, and who this man once was with his wife. Remi was the one here in the moment with Tucker now.

"For me too," she said to him, while their mouths parted again and were just inches apart.

"Are you sure it's not too soon?" he asked her, hoping his body would understand if she thought they were moving entirely too fast and wanted to wait.

Remi reached for the button and zipper on his denim. He felt eighteen years old again and worried about making this last. This woman had suddenly made him feel like there was going to be no turning back. He kissed her full on the mouth, and brought his wandering hand up further into her dress. He cupped a breast through her lacy bra. He wanted to see her, and feel more of her.

∞∞

Kate's black SUV rolled over the curb and onto Tucker's driveway. Countless times she had bounced over that curb, but now it was no longer her driveway, she thought, and then instantly wondered where Tucker's truck was at nine o'clock on a Saturday night. He always parked it on the driveway. Livy was asleep in the seat behind her, but picking up her blanket had to happen tonight, or no one would get any sound sleep once they were back home. *At Riley's place.* Kate was annoyed at Tucker for forgetting to pack the blanket with the rest of her things. She stepped down from the SUV in her red high heels to match her short skirt. She and Riley had gone out to dinner in St. Louis, and the teenage neighbor girl had watched Livy. Hiring a babysitter was not something Kate was comfortable doing yet. She thought about asking Tucker to keep Livy one more night, but Riley convinced her otherwise. Their evening, however, was cut short when Livy could not find her blanket at bedtime. She cried and threw a tantrum until the babysitter gave up trying to soothe her and inevitably called Kate.

The house was dark. Kate glanced out onto the street to be sure Tucker had not parked his truck there. There was nothing alongside of the road, but she instantly spotted his truck on the neighbor's driveway. She frowned at the oddity of that. She reached on the seat for her cell phone and noticed the text she sent Tucker had still not been answered. *So, he was with the neighbor?* Kate left the running vehicle on Tucker's driveway. She had to be quick, but she was going across the street to see if Tucker was inside of that house. Her red heels crushed the rocks on the road as she took long strides in the dark under a single street light. She reached the neighbor's front door, and only slightly hesitated before she rang the bell. Light shone through the closed window blinds on the house, which convinced Kate that she was not disturbing anyone too late.

Their limbs were entangled. Their clothes were coming off. And they were breathless when the doorbell startled them in the heat of heavy foreplay. Remi's eyes widened, and she quickly pulled down her dress to cover herself. Tucker struggled in a hurry to fasten his pants. "Are you expecting anyone this late?" he asked her.

"No!" she whispered, abruptly. "It has to be some sort of knock and run prank. I don't get visitors." With that, Kate rang the doorbell again.

"Let's answer it," Tucker stood up and initiated the move. He really didn't care who was at the door. He did, however, pick up on the fear of Remi's uncertainty, so he chose to take the initiative to protect her. Remi followed quickly behind him.

When Tucker swung open the door, he was beyond taken aback to see Kate on the other side. But he wasn't half as shocked as she was to see him standing there. Shirt unbuttoned and untucked. And his lips were pink. The kind of chapped color of pink Tucker's lips turned when he was making love.

"Kate! What are you doing?" Remi stood just a foot behind Tucker at her own front door, and she felt Kate's eyes on her right before she bore her angry eyes back into Tucker's.

"You forgot Livy's blanket. I need to get in the house. She's with me, asleep in the car."

"What? The one that she sleeps with? No. We rolled it up together, and shoved it into the front pocket of her backpack. She wanted it next to her socks."

"Are you kidding me? I just got called home from a dinner date when the babysitter was at her wits end about the conniption fit Livy was having over the missing blanket."

"Babysitter? Kate, I could have watched Livy tonight. You had a stranger come in?"

Kate was caught, but she didn't care. She was not going to run every single thing by Tucker. She and Riley had their own life now. "Obviously you had plans tonight," Kate said, sizing up Remi, barefoot in her black shift dress. She imagined Tucker's hands underneath that dress, and she wanted to throw up in her mouth.

"It was fine, Tucker," Kate all but spat at him. She was angry at what she was thinking. She had no right to be, but she was.

Tucker glanced at Remi. "I'll be right back," he told her, as he stepped outside when Kate started to walk away.

"Thanks for the tip on the blanket," Kate's tone was snarky. "You could have answered your cell phone and saved me the trip here." Her heels were loud on the concrete driveway before she made her way across the street with Tucker taking long strides to catch up to her. He stopped her at the end of his driveway.

"Wait! Before you get in your car and our voices wake Livy, I have something to say to you." Tucker was firm.

"Not now. I am way too pissed off at you!" Kate glared at him underneath the street light.

"For what? The blanket that I did pack after all? For not answering my cell phone because I was busy?"

"What are you doing with her, Tucker? Are you sleeping with her? Do you even know her?" Kate got right to the point of where her anger stemmed from.

"We went out to dinner," Tucker replied.

"And now you were about to have sex with her?"

"Kate, please."

"Fine. Go. I'm sorry I interrupted —obviously interrupted— your date." Kate stormed off in her loud heels, got into her vehicle, and backed up just inches past Tucker still standing on the curb. And yes, Remi was watching the entire scene from her living room window.

Chapter 8

Tucker walked back across the street, not at all certain with how he was feeling. Of all his emotions, confused won. Kate was clearly upset about the blanket, but even more so she appeared to be greatly affected by him being with Remi. He shook his head in annoyance as he reached Remi's front door, and she opened it for him before he attempted to let her know he had returned.

"Hey..." she said, as he stepped back into her house. "How awkward was that?"

"Yeah, but should it have been? I mean, really, my soon-to-be ex-wife fucked around on me for months. Sorry for my language..."

Remi waved a hand in front of her face. "It's fine. I understand why you're upset, but as you said, why was Kate so riled up over... um, us." *Were they an us?*

"I don't know," Tucker admitted. "I guess she was just caught off guard. I'm sorry she interrupted. I suppose I should have paid more attention to my phone vibrating in my pocket." As he spoke, they both thought about what they were in the process of doing with each other.

"I think you were a little preoccupied," Remi giggled, as they stood toe to toe in her living room. Their night together was ending, but they had bonded over food and sharing their personal stories. An effortless camaraderie had already formed between them.

"I liked being preoccupied with you," he admitted, but he never reached for her. Never touched her.

"Me too," she agreed.

"Kate killed the mood for tonight, though, didn't she?" he honestly stated, but a part of him wanted to fall into her again and whisk her off to her bedroom right now. Despite the interruption. Regardless of the fact that he was thinking too much right now. *Kate confused him. He was attracted to Remi. But he didn't want to hurt anyone.*

Remi shrugged. She looked down at her bare feet on the hardwood floor. Tucker still wore his pointed toe grey cowboy boots. She felt his open palm on the side of her cheek. And then he gently placed two of his fingers underneath her chin. His hands were large and thick. But his touch was tender. His fingers made her body feel tingly all over. She stood on her toes when he met her lips with his. He kissed her full on the mouth and she was entirely responsive. She wanted to find her voice and ask him, *to take her to bed,* but he eventually pulled away, leaving her breathless when he said, "I want to see you again."

∞∞

Kate quietly closed the door to Livy's bedroom. She was still asleep, even after Kate carried her inside from the parked vehicle in the triple-car garage. In the dark she managed to find the tightly rolled blanket squashed inside the backpack on the dresser top. She pushed away the thought of how Tucker was too busy tonight to text her back to tell her where he had put the blanket. She was terribly bothered by the fact that he had put someone else first. *Someone else.* Whether that woman meant anything to him or not, she had come before their daughter – and her. *Had she honestly expected Tucker to live the rest of his life alone?* Kate reminded herself that she was the one who wanted out of their marriage.

She walked up a second flight of stairs to get to the master bedroom. She didn't like the fact that Livy slept alone on an altogether different floor in the house. But when she told Riley as much, he shushed her concerns. *They needed their privacy. The house was equipped with a state-of-the-art security system. All was well. Let it go.*

Kate had her red strappy heels dangling from two fingers when she reached the open door of their master suite. Riley was lying on their uncovered bed, wearing only his black silk boxer shorts. His legs were crossed at the ankles, and he was looking up at the television high on the corner wall.

"Hi…" she caught his attention.

"You made it back. I hope you found the blanket," he said, and Kate thought she detected annoyance in his voice.

"I did," she said, not wanting to share anything about the evening – including where she found Tucker. And *who* he was with. And *what* he was doing.

"Why don't you come to bed," Riley suggested. "I need to sleep. I have an early meeting in the morning." Only Riley scheduled meetings on Sunday mornings. Work, for him, never stopped.

She stared at his narrow body frame. He didn't have an ounce of fat, or much muscle. He was a runner, not a weight lifter. The first time she saw him, his physique reminded her of the country music singer, Tim McGraw. His hands and feet were slender and narrow, unlike the thickness that Tucker had all over his entire body. He was more of a Garth Brooks body type, only with less pudge. This was the first time Kate had compared the two of them, in the privacy of her mind. There was a softness about Tucker when he made love to her. She had yet to find that with Riley. It was mind-blowing, satisfying sex with Riley. Pure and simple pleasure-seeking sex. But sometimes it was rough more so than gentle, and it felt more like assault than affection. *Why had she first realized that now? And what did this even mean as she and Tucker were on the verge of divorcing, and she was going to spend the rest of her life with Riley. He was a man of prestige and wealth. She could live like royalty, and never want for anything she couldn't previously afford.*

Kate walked over to the king-size bed and kissed him good night before he turned off the television in the bedroom they shared. She was grateful to him. He had already given her so much. And tonight, he was patient with her chasing after a blanket that she already unknowingly had in that house. She wanted to be with Riley tonight. Just like Tucker wanted to be with that woman across the street. But he claimed he needed sleep. So, Kate would stand in the steam from a hot shower and try to find some clarity about the changes in her life. And later, she would fall asleep next her new man. And she would try to forget how she missed the skin-on-skin contact, the soft caresses of making love. *Didn't every man want to kiss until his lips were a raw shade of pink?*

ꝏꝏ

It had been a long time since Tucker cooked a substantial breakfast on a Sunday morning. Livy was a typical picky eater for a toddler, and her mother chose to be finicky in an effort to not gain a single pound. A pan of homemade biscuits was browning in the oven, and the sausage gravy was bubbling in a skillet on the stovetop. He felt jittery and it was not because his stomach was empty. He was excited about cooking and surprising Remi.

He donned oven mitts on each hand, and then he made his way out of his house with a basket full of biscuits buried beneath paper towels, and a skillet full of sausage gravy. He felt a little nervous about showing up unexpectedly when he reached her front door. He used his elbow to ring the doorbell, and he hoped she wasn't a late sleeper. The last time he glanced at the clock in the kitchen when he was cooking it had been eight-twelve. It had to be close to nine o'clock by now, he thought. He heard footsteps on the opposite side of the door. When Remi opened it, Tucker grinned like a kid on Christmas.

"What are you doing? What have you done?" Remi asked, smiling, as she pulled back the paper towels from the basket to reveal the hot biscuits.

"Breakfast is served… if you're interested?"

Remi immediately stepped back to let Tucker inside of her house. She was not at all used to visitors, but Tucker was already so much more than someone to chit chat with. He followed her to the kitchen. She was wearing a pair of green plaid boxer shorts and a pink tank top, sans a bra. He assumed those were her pajamas, and he felt his body tighten at the thought of seeing her in such a personal state. She wore no makeup and her hair was in a high, messy knot on top of her head.

Once their hands were free, Tucker stood near the kitchen counter with Remi. She thought of how she had never seen him wear anything but denim. He was wearing faded jeans again now with a red t-shirt. His matching red tennis shoes made her smile.

"I made coffee… or I have milk or OJ." They didn't know a thing about each other's likes or dislikes yet.

"I don't drink coffee," he admitted, "but I'm good with milk. Have you eaten anything yet this morning?"

Remi smiled. "Nope. I've been awake long enough to start the coffee, brush my teeth, and wash my face." She felt a little self-conscious in her pajamas in front of him, but after how close they had gotten last night, she pushed the embarrassed feeling out of her mind.

He thought she looked sexy first thing in the morning. "I wanted to do something nice for you since last night ended on sort of a disappointing note." He was referring to Kate's interruption, but Remi's mind flashed to the seductive goodnight kiss he gave her.

"This is sinful, you know that, right?" Remi retrieved two plates for them, and she anticipated eating a heaping plate of biscuits smothered in hot sausage gravy.

"In what way?" Tucker asked.

"We all have that one food that we cannot get enough of when we are eating it, so we purposely try to avoid it on a regular basis. That, for me, is b's and g's."

Tucker laughed out loud. "Well I obviously had no idea, but now I'm super happy I didn't make bacon and eggs." They both laughed.

After they dipped their forks into their food, Tucker caught himself staring at her while she ate. Remi reached for her napkin, in case she had food on her face.

"I like this, being here like this, with you," Tucker told her what was on his mind. "This is the second meal we've shared and it's refreshing to see a woman not afraid to eat."

"Oh great, suddenly I feel like a piggy," Remi put her fork down.

"Stop. That's not what I meant. I like food, and it's good to see you do, too."

"Within moderation," she attempted to defend her hefty appetite. "I mean, I at least try not to bust out of my clothes sometimes."

Tucker smiled. "You look beautiful exactly the way you are." Last night she was dressed to the nines, and this morning she looked all-natural. Tucker truly saw all of her beauty.

"You are too much, Tucker Brandt. Only days ago you were a stranger to me, just a new neighbor who I saw as a nice guy."

"And now? What do you see?" he was egging her on.

"Oh I see more of good thing," she began, feeling giddy. "You are sexy as hell, not that I didn't see that from the get go." They both laughed out loud.

"You stole my word," Tucker interjected.

"Yeah?" she grinned.

"I'm not taking back beautiful, but sexy was my first choice." Tucker pointed his fork at her and then dug into his food again. Remi's smile lit up her entire face, as she had this feeling overcome her of never having enjoyed a compliment more. And then she too started to eat again. This was one plate of food that she was going to indulge in and finish.

∞∞

Tucker offered to take the dirty dishes back to his house, but Remi insisted on washing them in her kitchen. They stood together at the sink, as if they were a couple or something. And at one point, Tucker saw Remi smiling.

"What?"

"I'm just thinking," she answered.

"About me naked?"

She howled with laughter. "Well, that too…" He smirked as she continued. "I was thinking how I'll bet we are already getting the neighbors talking. Last night with your truck on my drive and your ex-wife at my door." Tucker thought how Kate was not yet his ex-wife. But close enough. And somehow the thought of that, of her, had hurt a little less. "And then this morning the image of you running across the street with kitchenware." She giggled louder.

Tucker threw the dish towel in his hand on top of the counter. He wanted both hands free for this. He moved closer to her. Her hands were wet from the sudsy dish water in the sink in front of her. She turned to face him, dripping water onto the floor. He took both of her hands in his and he pressed hers to his chest. His t-shirt was now wet. He pulled her closer. "Then let's give them a reason to talk..." Tucker stated, and kissed her full on the lips. She deepened the kiss before he did, and he already wasn't confident that he could walk away from her again without being with her in the full sense. He wanted her.

He touched her breasts through the thin tank top she wore. He reached beneath it for more of her as he continued to kiss her hard and full on the mouth. The intensity of their passion was overwhelming them.

"I want to make love to you, please Tucker, touch me..." Remi heard herself say those words and she wondered how being so closed off from the world had suddenly transformed into feeling such ease with another human being. She wanted this man in so many ways. She liked who she had already become with him. Instantaneously, she allowed him in. She had taken him to a place in her heart that nobody had been. Not even those before him that she believed she loved – and trusted.

"Take me to your bed," he told her in between kisses and losing clothing along the way. When they reached the end of the hallway, Remi backed him into her bedroom and gently pushed him down on the foot end of the unmade bed. She stepped out of her girly boxer shorts. He had already removed her tank top. She stood there naked in front of this man. Pesky self-consciousness sunk into her mind, but she prompted herself to recall that Tucker thought her curves and the fullness of her body were sexy. He reached for her. His shirt was off, and his jeans needed to come off. He stood up in front of her and she made the first move to take off the rest of his clothing. Barefoot in jeans was a sexy look on him. When his jeans were at his ankles, his underwear soon followed. They stood touching, pressing themselves together, and driving each other to the brink. Skin on skin. And then he laid her down on the bed. He found her core. She reacted. "God, Tucker, please. Now." There was something unbelievably sexy how she begged for him. He found her with his mouth and he showed her no mercy. Her world was still spinning on its ecstasy axis when he slowly entered her and rocked over her. Her fingers dug into the thick skin on his back. His thrusts became more intense and he called out her name, once, twice – and finally. Tucker buried his head in her bare chest. Remi's thoughts reeled. *Was this just sex between them? Absolutely incredible sex. Were they friends with benefits? Two lonely people finding comfort in physical intimacy? Or would they both want something more?* Remi didn't have an answer, because all of this happened unbelievably fast. And people just didn't stick around in her life. Tucker's reaction came much sooner than she expected when he caressed her face with the soft palm of his hand, and then she heard him say, "I'm free falling for you."

Chapter 9

"What did you just say?" Remi asked, even though she clearly heard his every word. Perhaps she was buying herself some time to react to what he said to her.

Tucker was close to her, and he stayed so. His hand brushed the hair away from covering the side of her face. There was nothing between them but rumpled sheets. Their bodies were bare, and he felt something for this woman that he was not about to ignore, or play down as only a physical need. "I'm falling hard and fast. There's a connection between us, and it's more than just a physical attraction." Tucker wanted to get to know her better, but he knew he had to use caution. He didn't want to overwhelm her. She was still a guarded girl. He could see it in her eyes now, the uncertainty.

Remi tugged on what she could of the sheet between them. She attempted to cover her bare chest. It was a barrier for her. "There is something here," she admitted, "but if I'm being honest —and that's so easy to do with you— I'm afraid." She left her words end at that. She wasn't exactly afraid of losing him, because she didn't really have him. Sex had never meant possession to her. And furthermore, Remi survived a broken heart before. *Maybe this time she wouldn't fall in heart first?*

"I know," Tucker responded. "It's like a whirlwind for me right now. I'm getting a divorce. I'm missing my little girl in that house across the street. I never expected to feel this way this fast. I mean, I was not looking for you, or for this." *This* was in reference to getting laid.

Remi nodded. "Let's agree on something," she began. "Not to define this. If you're not going to leave my bed and never look back, if you want to see where this goes… I think I do too." That was as candid and straight-forward as Remi could be right now. Tucker was still very much connected to the family he just lost. She saw the way he responded to Kate last night. He still cared about her, and her feelings. He was on the rebound. *Instant rebound.* Remi, however, believed that she was long over Sam Malone and their broken engagement. She was just hurt and closed off now. But Tucker made it downright impossible for her to emotionally shut down. And that was entirely new to her.

"The last thing I want to do is never look back," Tucker spoke truthfully, and he wanted to lunge himself toward her and kiss her full and hard. But he was being cautious with her feelings in the aftermath of their sudden intimacy. "I agree to your terms. Let's just be and see where this goes."

Remi smiled. "Does this feel the least bit insane to you?"

"It does, but it doesn't," Tucker chuckled.

"Yeah, I know what you mean," Remi agreed, and she initiated the kiss shared between them that quickly escalated to other passionate things.

∞∞

Tucker was lost in thought. Being with her. He was completely taken in. *Her mind. Her body.* He could listen to Remi talk for hours. Her alto voice soothed him when she spoke, and when she called out his name in the midst of their private ecstasy together, he was a goner.

He stood in the kitchen of his home, and his eyes met the stapled stack of divorce papers on the counter that he had yet to sign. He would though. Because he had to. There wasn't a choice. Kate moved on. And when he was with Remi, Tucker just now mused, he didn't think about his broken life.

The front door to the house swung open without warning. Brothers never knocked. "In the kitchen, Chase!" Tucker called out. His older brother smiled wide, as he rounded the corner. He stopped on the opposite end of the island from where Tucker stood. Both wore jeans, but Chase didn't fill his out like Tucker did. *Chase was lean, Tucker was meaty*, as their mother used to say. Only eighteen months apart, and so vastly different.

"Hey," Chase said. "What are you up to?"

"Nothing right now. I just got in a little while ago." That was the truth. It was early evening, and he had been with Remi all day since breakfast.

"Oh yeah? Where'd you go?" Chase was actually curious. He hoped his brother wouldn't say Rix Hardware. No one worked on a Sunday if it could be avoided. But he knew his brother had to somehow pass this newfound time on his hands.

Tucker paused. "I wasn't going to put this out there, just yet, so I would appreciate if what I tell you would stay between us. Got it?"

Chase held his breath. Of course his brother could tell him anything in confidence. He just momentarily wished to God that he and Kate were not for some-off-the-wall-reason getting back together. Tucker was like a yo-yo to her. He was putty in her hands. And Chase was tired of seeing him get played for a fool. But Kate had his heart, and Tucker would likely overlook her transgressions and take her back if she were to change her mind about the divorce. Chase knew his brother well and was absolutely certain of that.

"I wasn't looking. The thought was the farthest thing from my mind," Tucker started out. "You know me. I'm not a player or some kind of party guy who's out to have a good time." Tucker was not prepared to talk about this, and he wondered if he should switch gears before it was too late, and just not say anything about Remi yet. But he knew Chase would press him. "I took the woman across the street out for dinner and drinks."

Chase chuckled. "Are you serious?" He recalled when he jokingly commented the last time he was there about the then-mysterious neighbor lady being *hot*.

"We hit it off," Tucker defended himself. "Long story short. Our other neighbor, Joy crashed into Remi's mailbox – and I set her up with a new one at Rix. She needed help installing it, so I offered."

"And then you asked her out?" Chase frowned. His brother wasn't even divorced yet, but he couldn't honestly blame him. Kate left him. He was a free man.

"Sort of. As I said, we get along. She's fun, she's smart, and she's sexy."

"Oh? So did you kiss her?" Chase assumed not, but he had to ask.

Tucker grinned.

Chase's eyes widened.

Tucker laughed out loud.

Chase quizzed him, "You didn't? Already, man? Holy shit, good for you!"

"It's not what you think," Tucker spoke in his defense and Remi's. "I really like her. We didn't just have sex, if you know what I mean. I care about her. I want to be close to her again."

Chase refrained from reacting. He wanted to tell his little brother that he had lost his mind. *No one falls for someone in a matter of days. Had he seriously believed he was in love with another woman already, just days after his wife and child moved out?*

"You need to slow down," Chase spoke his thoughts regardless. And he wasn't referring to sex. "Have a good time with her, but don't put your heart on the line already."

"This isn't about getting laid," Tucker was quick to speak up. "I know how I feel."

"You didn't tell her that, did you?" Chase all but held his breath.

"I did." Tucker was not afraid to be honest with anyone.

"Oh God." Chase rolled his eyes.

"I didn't tell you this for you to judge me. I know how crazy it may sound, but it's happening. I'm falling in love again."

"So you've fallen out of love with Kate? If you have, that's news to me." Chase was being harsh.

"Kate's not mine to love anymore." Those words saddened Tucker, but the fact was it didn't hurt so much anymore.

"Someone is going to get hurt," Chase spoke as if he was the adult forewarning a child.

"I'm a big boy," Tucker defended himself yet again.

"That you are," Chase stated. "I want to see you happy, I do. I just want you to have time to adjust to this major change in your life before you take on the world with someone new."

"I am happy when I'm with Remi. I just want to enjoy that feeling right now, and you know, we'll see where it goes."

Chase understood. "I hear you," he said. "At least you no longer have blue balls."

They chuckled in unison, and Tucker offered his big brother a beer because he knew he definitely needed one.

Chapter 10

Kate was at the paralegal office in downtown St. Louis on Market Street, a company that she had been a part of for almost a decade. Rose Trimble held the door for her as she climbed the wide concrete steps in quick motion in heels. "Thanks Rosie," Kate spoke, and Rose laughed out loud. No one else except Kate called her Rosie.

"How are you, honey?" Rose asked, in her typical motherly way. She was aware of the changes in Kate's life in recent months. Everyone in that office witnessed the instantaneous flirtatious chemistry between the new lawyer in town and Kate. When Riley Ratchford bought a house on the other side of the Mississippi River in O'Fallon, Illinois, they all perceived his intentions were to break up a marriage, and a young family. Rose knew his kind. And she worried that Kate, in time, would regret her dire actions. *Money and the high life weren't everything.*

"I'm well. You?" Kate's long blonde hair reached halfway down her back today. She wore a black business suit with an appropriate above-the-knee-length skirt.

"Wonderful for a Monday. The weekend went too fast as usual."

Kate nodded, and agreed, especially since Riley had worked the entire morning on Sunday. The only time they spent together lately were dinner meetings. He included her, and she relished in dressing up and delving into the social setting, but time alone together and with Livy was something Riley seemed to be avoiding since they moved in with him. It was just a feeling Kate had. *She could be wrong. Living together was an adjustment for all of them.*

"I thought for a moment yesterday morning that I was going to see you with Riley," Rose began, as they walked in unison through the lobby, where all glass windowed walls surrounded them. Kate looked at her, puzzled, and Rose explained. "I was at the City Coffee House and Creperie for breakfast. Riley was there. He had some sort of meeting, it looked like from afar. I never spoke to him."

"He did have a business meeting yesterday," Kate confirmed, and what Rose said made sense to her now. She wasn't aware that it was a breakfast meeting. Riley never shared that information with her.

"Kate, can I tell you something in confidence?" Rose asked, and the two of them stopped walking part way through the lobby. Before they separated on their quest to get to their separate offices this morning, Kate listened after she assured Rose that *her secret was safe.* "Well it's not my secret, and I'm not really even sure if it's a secret at all. Riley may have told you." Rose set the stage for this conversation piece. *It was about Riley.*

"Told me what?"

"The man he met with yesterday was John Isenhower, the dean of Principia School here in St. Louis."

"So, he needs a lawyer for something?" Kate asked, and she assumed that his case would make its way to her desk.

Rose shrugged. "My husband and I were eating when the two of them left. The dean stopped at a table near ours to talk to someone, and I overheard his conversation. He was asked about enrollment, and John Isenhower mentioned how it's soaring. He stated that between the two campuses, enrollment is in the thousands, and they gain new students regularly."

Kate was quickly losing interest in this story. She couldn't have cared less about the enrollment at the local campus. If there was one thing that she and Tucker completely agreed upon, it was the education that Livy would get within the O'Fallon school system.

"That's great," Kate heard herself say, and her tone blared uninterested.

"There's more," Rose added. "The dean's exact words were that he, in fact, just wrapped up a meeting with a potential new enrollee — a three-year-old."

"What?" Her mind registered quickly where Rose was now going with this. "Livy?"

Rose nodded.

"Like hell," Kate stated. She couldn't believe this. *Riley had gone behind her back to line up a new school for Livy? He was not her parent.*

"I didn't want to upset you," Rose looked torn, "but because you were not at that meeting, I had a feeling you didn't know. She's your child, Kate. Don't let that new, charming man in your life bully you into making too many more drastic changes."

"Bully?" Kate spoke. That seemed harsh.

"Forgive me if I've overstepped. I just call it like I see it." Rose squeezed Kate's arm and walked away. Their conversation may have concluded, but the subject matter was far from over.

ꝏꝏ

Kate sat at her desk in front of a dark computer monitor. She had not even powered it on. Work was the farthest thing from her mind. She was upset with Riley. *When had he planned to tell her about his intentions? Had he really wanted to send Livy to a boarding school? She was still a baby for chrissakes! Her baby. Tucker's baby. Not his. Riley was out of line.* Her hands were trembling. This was the man she gave up her marriage for. She uprooted Livy from the only home she knew. She broke Tucker's heart. *What if Riley wasn't the man she believed him to be?* Regret sunk hard and fast into Kate's heart.

ꝏꝏ

The first thing Remi did when she walked into her private guidance office at school was reread the text Tucker had sent her this morning.

Have dinner with me tonight. My place. I'll cook.

Yesterday morning it was her place, and he also cooked. And what happened afterward, and throughout most of their lazy Sunday, was still front and center on Remi's mind. Tucker had said it first. *He was falling for her.* And Remi certainly knew the feeling. Yes, things were moving ridiculously fast between them, but neither one knew how to slow the emotions down.

She finally texted him back.

I'd like that! I'll come over after work. I can help cook.

It had been a long time since Remi had something to look forward to, someone to be with, and to share her time. She liked that feeling more than she wanted to admit. She didn't want to get hurt again. The walls she put up around her heart had suddenly and unexpectedly come crashing down – at Tucker's hand. She wanted to take a chance on him. Her heart told her to jump in, and she had. But her mind was protectively proceeding with caution.

Tucker responded to her reply.

Looking forward to it! I hope you have a good day. You already made mine.

Without hesitation, Remi agreed.

∞∞

Tucker swaggered through the hardware store like he was eighteen again. *That woman.* She made him feel things he had not felt in a very long time. If ever. There was no pretense with Remi. *What you saw was what you got.* She let Tucker into her guarded heart. And now there was so much more he wanted to discover about her.

∞∞

Riley stepped into Kate's office and closed the door. She was minutes from taking a lunch break. She planned to go outside for a walk. She wasn't hungry, and she desperately needed the fresh air to clear her mind. Although she knew a change of scenery would not be a cure all.

"Hello beautiful," he spoke, as he walked across the room to her. "Remember the first time we made love, in here, right there on that desktop?" He grinned, a little slyly, and Kate only stared at him. *Made love? Love? Was that what they were doing? Did she truly love him – or merely the life that he could offer her?*

"I remember," she responded, with very little emotion on her face. "I thought then that we had this connection. An undeniable chemistry. I could see your soul and you could see mine. I banked on that. I abandoned so much of my life to start anew with you."

Riley nodded. He instantly picked up on her strange demeanor. "You okay?"

"I don't know," she answered truthfully. "I heard something secondhand this morning and it's been on my heart for hours." Riley listened raptly. The seriousness of her tone had captured his attention. "Do you know a John Isenhower, by chance?" Kate got right to the point.

Riley teetered back and forth on his heels. He slipped both of his hands in the front pockets of his dark suit pants. "Yes, as a matter of fact, I do. He's well-known in this city. The dean of Principia, right?"

"Apparently he is. I had no idea about him, and really didn't have an interest in him or his campus. It seems that you feel otherwise though. Unless you are hiding a secret child from me, I can only assume that you were planning ahead for my daughter to attend a private boarding school now or in time to come?"

Riley looked uneasy. He was not used to a woman calling him out. None of his previous relationships progressed for that very reason. He was attracted to headstrong women, but they needed to keep their assertiveness in check when pertaining to him. "I don't have any children," he began. "But yes, I was looking ahead for what might be in Livy's best interest as she gets a little older."

Kate held her breath for a long moment before responding. "You know all there is to know about my life, my child, and what her father and I want for her future. You bought a house in the City of O'Fallon because of me, and us. The three of us are going to have a future together. Stop me if I'm wrong…"

Riley clenched his jaw and loudly cleared his throat. "We can have this discussion at home."

"Nope. It's happening right now," Kate stated, holding her own. "Explain to me what in the hell you were thinking. One, you kept this from me. And two, you were way out of line."

Riley nodded. "You're overreacting. You're upset over something that doesn't even have to happen. I was just researching our options."

"Options to get rid of Livy? I thought you knew that she and I are a packaged deal. If you want me, she comes with." Kate paused before she choked on her words. She had yet to see Riley hit it off with Livy. He rarely made any attempt to try with her. Was this the kind of man, father-figure, that she wanted in her child's life? Kate was utterly disgusted with herself for being blindsided by him. *His charm. His wealth. His prestige.*

"Hey now, calm down, beautiful," Riley walked around the desk to be closer to her. He bent to his knees in front of her chair. He grabbed the arms of it to swivel it in his direction. "That's not what I was doing. I never mentioned it to you because it's not something that has to happen. Livy is adorable. She's yours. I'm just honored to be a part of her life because of you. I love you, Katherine." Kate momentarily closed her eyes so Riley would not see the tears behind them. "Come on..." Riley put a hand on one of her bare knees. He gently rubbed it with his open palm. Kate watched him. She doubted him – and them. "I'm sorry. I would never purposely bully you into doing anything you are not comfortable with."

Bully. There was that word again. Kate felt uneasy, but she didn't let it show. Riley moved closer to her and he kissed her lightly on the lips. She hesitated to respond. She was still upset with him. And hurt by his deceit. He moved his lips over hers more aggressively. And this time she felt compelled to react. She opened her mouth on his. Riley Ratchford had a way of getting what he wanted. And now, right at this moment, he wanted Kate Brandt.

Chapter 11

Remi did a quick change of clothes after work from a dress to her favorite black cropped leggings and a white v-neck t-shirt with a little pocket over the left breast. She slipped into black flip flops and felt giddy as she crossed the street to Tucker's house. It was odd that she had never been inside of his house. He had been in hers. And she was in his truck. And he had been in her bed. The thought of what he planned to make for dinner crossed her mind, but she really didn't care what they ate. She just wanted to be with him. She wouldn't say it, but she had missed him and thought of him practically nonstop since they had been together just the day before.

She rang the doorbell and he answered a few seconds later, in jeans and white socks and still wearing his Rix Hardware polo shirt. This one was black. "Hi there," Tucker welcomed her inside of his house. The hardwood flooring caught her eye immediately. It was authentic hardwood, not like the laminate she had all throughout her house. The place was modernized, and definitely had a woman's touch – even though that woman didn't live there anymore. Kate had expensive taste. Leather furniture. Cherrywood coffee and end tables.

Remi wanted to say it was all beautiful, but she feared that would be a credit to Kate, so she kept quiet. "Something smells delicious already," she told him, and a part of her was tempted to lean in to greet him with a kiss. But she didn't. Tucker did reach out to take her hand. "Follow me into the kitchen and I'll show you."

He was baking marinated prime rib, while wild rice and greens were already prepared.

"Seriously? I thought I was going to help cook, you know, like boil the pasta or something?"

Tucker grinned. He had let go of her hand when they reached the center of the kitchen and stood at the island. "You like pasta?"

"I do. I'm just implying that you didn't have to go through so much trouble for me..."

"I love to eat," he defended himself, "and cooking for one is no fun. I'm enjoying this, with you." His open palm caressed the side of her face. She momentarily closed her eyes. His touch was both gentle and seductive. Remi placed her hand on top of his that held her face. "Can I get you a glass of wine or something?"

She nodded. "Yes, please. Today was a busy one in guidance, and I could have used the alcohol at noon already."

Tucker chuckled as he parted from her and went to the refrigerator for that bottle of wine he bought earlier at the grocery store. "Serious problems among our youth, huh?"

Remi sighed. "One, in particular, he's an extremely bright, gifted kid, but his home life isn't the best – and it's bringing him down. He will not admit it, but I've picked up on it with how often he stops into my office and the things he talks about. The way he mentions his mother in rehab who he visits only every other weekend. His dad now has a new girlfriend," Remi explained, of course leaving out Crue's name. Tucker poured them each a glass of white wine and handed her one. She took a long sip from the stemless glass before continuing. "He comes to see me daily. Today he talked past his twenty minutes allotted. He's worried about his mom finding out about the new woman in his dad's life. He thinks it will send her off course from her treatment."

"So are his parents divorced?" Tucker asked, feeling grateful that Livy was only a toddler and the changes in their lives were something she would grow up accustomed to.

"Yes," Remi answered, realizing that their stories were a little bit parallel. Kate had not seemed too fond of her either when she found Tucker at her home in an obviously disheveled state. But Kate wasn't a child. She was Tucker's ex. "It's hard on kids at any age, I suppose."

"I was just thinking that actually. In one way, I'm glad Livy is still little and seems to be adjusting to our separate lives."

Remi nodded. "I hope to see her again soon."

"I'll have her tomorrow for two nights." Tucker smiled. "I want her to spend some time with you, with us together, I mean."

"I'd like that," Remi said, "but I know you need your time alone with her as well."

"I never thought it would be like this," Tucker began.

"Raising your child in separate homes?" Remi was looking for clarification.

"Yes that, and this," Tucker said, reaching for her hand. "I don't feel so alone and lost when I'm with you. I want to balance being a dad, and getting to know you better. I want this time with you. I like this new and different direction that my life is taking."

Remi laughed before she spoke in return. "It's a whirlwind, isn't it? These feelings, I mean. It's like we've known each other long before now. Is that ridiculous to say?"

"Not at all," Tucker responded. "You've said what I'm thinking. I want what we are doing to keep happening."

"Me too," Remi smiled. "I'm drawn to your honesty. You just outright tell me how you're feeling. I'm not sure I've ever had a relationship like that before. It's refreshing. It's what I do. All day long… tell me what you are feeling… share what's on your mind, or heavy on your heart."

"You wanna know what I'm thinking?" Tucker asked her, and she giggled a little, as he continued. "I'm thinking that we still have thirty minutes of cook time left for the meat."

"That's a long time," Remi played along.

"It is." He finished off the wine in his glass, and she took another long sip of her own. When she set her glass down on the countertop of the island, she looked at him with desire in her eyes. He stepped closer to her and kissed her long and slow on the lips. Remi's entire body responded to him.

Her back was pressed up against the island. Tucker's body was against hers. It was early evening. It was still daylight outside. There were no guidelines with them. They could fall into bed together before dinner. Their relationship was brand new and exciting. And they wanted to tear each other's clothes off.

An abruptly opened front door and little feet on the hardwood stopped them both instantly. They pulled away from each other, both wide-eyed. Tucker made his way through the kitchen just as Livy ran to him. He picked her up immediately after she called out, *daddy!* And then he saw Kate walking through the living room. Dressed to the nines, heels and all, and clearly straight from work.

"What's going on?" he spoke first. "Do I have my days mixed up? I thought you were coming tomorrow?" Tucker smiled happily at his little girl, concealing how unnerved he felt with her mother. He knew he hadn't confused his days. It would not have mattered as much if Remi wasn't there. But she was. And Kate needed to be respectful of his privacy now. That felt odd of him to think, but it was true. *He was moving on.*

"No mix up," Kate said, as she unapprovingly eyed Remi, who had just walked through the kitchen to join them. "Hi," Kate greeted her first, awkwardly.

"Hello Kate," Remi responded, in an attempt to sound friendly.

"Remi! Come see my room! Did daddy show you?"

Remi smiled. "No, I have not seen your bedroom." Kate smugly thought to herself, *but I'll bet you've seen Tucker's.*

"I want to show her, daddy!" Tucker winked at Remi, and the intimate, loving gesture did not go unnoticed by Kate.

"Go ahead," Tucker told them. He wanted Remi to feel comfortable in his home, despite the fact that Kate was there.

When they walked out of the kitchen together, Tucker creased his brow at Kate. "What are you doing?"

"Livy asked to see you when I picked her up from after-school care. I told her she had to wait until tomorrow and she got upset. I thought what would be the harm in stopping by for a few minutes before dinnertime? I had no idea you would be in the middle of something again."

"It's fine," Tucker stated, trying to conceal his irritability. He and Remi were once again interrupted by Kate. It didn't get much more awkward than that. *Twice!*

"Are you two seeing each other?" Kate wanted to ask if it was exclusive between them, if they had slept together. It was one thing to have a dinner date on a Saturday night, but this was a weeknight and she couldn't deny the pink, chapped lips of his again. *So they were making out in the kitchen?* She saw their wine glasses on the island. *Since when did Tucker enjoy drinking wine?*

"We are getting to know each other, Kate," Tucker spoke as a matter of fact.

"Okay," she threw up her hands. "You have every right. I just didn't think you would take to bed the first woman who came along." Kate rolled her eyes, and Tucker fumed.

"Really, Kate?" Tucker called her out for acting as if she was the innocent one in this. "I want you to call the next time you are planning to come over unannounced. And please stop passing judgement on Remi and myself. I care about her. Just like you care about Riley." That stung. And Tucker meant for it to. *Her relationship with Riley ruined their marriage.* Right now, Kate still had lingering anger toward Riley. And she felt torn. She was actually the one who wanted to see Tucker tonight. A part of her wanted to tell him about Principa School, and how terribly Riley had overstepped. *Livy was their daughter.* She wanted someone on her side with this, and she knew Tucker would be. But now Kate would not bring it up, as he was about to have dinner —and probably so much more— *with the woman he cared about.*

Livy's bedroom was located at the front of the house. Remi peeked out the window and told Livy that she could see her own house across the street. Livy giggled, and just as Remi was about to look away, she saw a car pull up on her driveway. She didn't recognize the blue coupe, so she waited and watched to see when the driver got out of it. She caught her breath when she saw Crue.

He was a student. He had no excuse for looking up her home address, and showing up on her doorstep. Remi was momentarily relieved that she was not home. Her job would be on the line if anyone were to witness them together outside of school. Remi felt uneasy. She never took her eyes off of him. He rang her doorbell. He stood and waited. Obviously he would have to leave when no one answered the door. A part of Remi thought to run over there and reem him for showing up. But she believed it was best not to.

Crue did eventually leave her property, and soon after Kate and Livy left Tucker's house as well. Remi could see in Tucker's eyes how difficult it was to say goodbye to his little girl. Sometimes short, unexpected visits could go either way and momentarily feed the soul, or leave you missing someone a million times more because the meeting wasn't long enough.

Tucker closed and locked the door behind them. Remi was in the kitchen, taking the prime rib out of the oven. The timer had gone off just minutes ago.

"I'm sorry about that," Tucker spoke.

"No need to be. She's your little girl. She wanted to see you. I enjoyed the time spent with her in her room, too."

Tucker smiled. "I was referring to Kate, and yet another one of her interruptions."

"She does appear to be unnerved by the idea of us," Remi stated.

"Well she will get used to it, seeing us together, I mean." Tucker stepped closer to her.

"That sounds nice," Remi told him.

"How hungry are you right now?' he asked her, and she giggled.

"Do you have any aluminum foil?"

Tucker pulled open a drawer and took the initiative to cover the meat on the stovetop. "There. It can wait," he stated, slyly.

"But you can't?" she teased, as he pulled her into his arms and kissed her hungrily on the mouth. Again, her body responded to him. She didn't need food and water to survive. She needed Tucker Brandt.

Tucker led her to his bedroom. She never asked if the rose-colored sheets he laid her down on was the same bedding he once shared with his wife. She didn't need to know because that was irrelevant. Remi was the woman in his arms now. She pulled her hair out of the tie that held together her messy bun after work. It fell onto her bare shoulders. Their clothes were strewn across the bedroom floor. Tucker's hands were on her body. And hers were on his. This wasn't merely passion and arousal between them. They were making love to each other, and discovering everything about their bodies. Together. And in sync. Tucker had already fallen in love, and Remi was teetering on the brink. All she had to do was allow it to happen. He entered her. His size took her breath. And their worlds collided. This was exactly where they both wanted to be.

Chapter 12

When Kate drove away from the house, she fought the image that haunted her mind. *Tucker and Remi*. He had every right to move on with his life. She couldn't expect him to live like a monk. She certainly hadn't. *Then why had it bothered her so much?*

Kate and Livy ate dinner alone. And it was after Livy's bedtime when Riley finally came home. Kate never texted or called him to reach out. She was still angry, and her anger at him mounted when he didn't get in touch with her tonight. *Letting someone know you're going to be late was a common courtesy.*

Kate was in the living area of their three-story home with twenty-foot high ceilings. She sat with her legs curled underneath her on one end of the white sectional. She was drinking her second glass of wine when Riley walked in. He spotted her, sitting near the solely lit lamp in that immense room. "All alone?" he asked.

"Liv's asleep. You're rather late, don't you think?" Her tone was cold.

"I am," he agreed. "I had somewhere to stop once I left the office."

"Somewhere? Another secret to keep from me?" She thought she saw Riley smirk. He walked over to her and knelt down on the floor in front of her. For a moment, she refused to look at him.

"When you have a good thing and you feel like it's slipping away from you, something happens," he started to explain. "It's like an alarm goes off, and panic sets in. It's do or die. Or you lose it all. I had that feeling today in your office. I broke your trust in me. I saw the doubt in your eyes." Kate was looking at him now. His blond hair and blue eyes. He was almost forty years old, but even in a designer suit and tie he still could look so boyish at times. His words to her were sincere. She owed him a listen. "I never should have done what I did. Livy is your child. I was being selfish. I don't have you all to myself anymore. I'm not complaining. I'm a big boy, and I'll deal. I'm sorry that I hurt you, Kate."

He never touched her. He only remained on his knees in front of her as a way, she assumed, to beg for a little mercy. She saw the man she fell for again. He was back. Or maybe she just allowed herself to see him again. The stress of leaving behind her old life, and Tucker, had gotten to her lately. Riley was her future. *He's who she chose,* Kate reminded herself of that now.

She reached for his face with her hands. And he in turn covered her hands with his own. He brought her fingers to his lips. "I love you, Katherine. I want to be with you for the rest of my life. Livy too. He released her hands and reached into his pants pocket. He held a small black velvet box. Kate covered her mouth with her hand. She knew this was coming. One day. But his timing was damn near perfect tonight. She needed his commitment. She wanted reassurance that they were going to be okay, that she had made the right decision in leaving her husband for him.

He flipped open the small lid to reveal a four-carat princess-cut diamond on a thick gold band. "Marry me, Katherine. Let's start the rest of our lives together. Commit to me, and love me as much as I love you."

Kate was crying. She wanted to say yes more than anything. And so she did.

She bent forward and watched him put the diamond on her finger. She was drawn to the finer things in life, and Riley Ratchford was at the helm of it all. She kissed him full on the mouth, and he beamed. *She was going to be his wife.* He had waited a very long time to have a woman as beautiful as Kate as his own. He started to unbutton her blouse. She reacted to what he was initiating right then and there. He pulled her down to the floor with him. He hardly kissed her at all. Their lovemaking was eager and almost rushed at times. Half of their clothes were still on their bodies when Riley took her with force. And while he was inside her, he told her to come for him. She managed to make it seem like a climax was actually happening to her body, and finally Riley released himself in turn. And when it was over, Kate's very first thought was *I never had to fake it with Tucker.*

She held out her hand and admired the oversized diamond ring, as Riley lay on the floor spent beside her. *This is my new life now,* Kate told herself.

ooo

"Crue?" Remi spoke as she saw the senior at O'Fallon Township High School peek his head through the open doorway of her office. Right on time as it was the start of his sixth hour class. He confidently walked in and closed the door behind him.

He never looked any different. He typically wore faded jeans, t-shirts, leather flip-flops on his feet. His dark hair was medium length, with some curl, and his bangs were always in his eyes. Brushing them away with one hand was a nervous habit for him, Remi often thought. He appeared calm and cool, but Remi sometimes sensed that was a cover. He had serious issues haunting his home life, and while Remi thought he was coping well considering it all, she had some doubt surface ever since the night before when she peered out of the window from across the street to her own house – and saw him. He had crossed a boundary between counselor and student. And that bothered her to no end. Most of all because she wanted to understand why.

"What's been going on with you?" she asked him as he plopped down in the chair in front of her desk. He always sat in the same one directly in front of her. Remi chalked that up to routine. We were all creatures of habit.

Crue shrugged. "I'm annoyed and angry."

"At who, or what?" Remi always pushed for the specifics.

"People who say they are going to be there for me, but when it comes down to crunch time, they're nowhere to be found." Crue didn't make fleeting eye contact like many of the teenagers who've stepped foot in her office, and this time was no different. His eyes bore into Remi's. She stared back.

"Are you referring to your dad?" Remi asked. "Because in your mom's defense, she can't be there for you right now at any given moment. I'm assuming she has not checked herself out of rehab?"

"You ask too many questions at once," Crue spat. He was angry. And it was new for Remi to see this from him. She always thought of Crue as one of two things. Either very good at covering up his emotions, or a master at keeping his feelings in check and not letting too much affect him.

"It's me you're angry with, isn't it?" Remi pressed him. Crue wasn't aware, but Remi had watched him stop by her house and leave. She wondered if he was upset that she was not there for him then, which was completely ridiculous because she could not meet with him off the school premises. A female high school employee and a male student meeting at her home would undoubtedly cause a scandal that her career would never survive if any preposterous rumors were to get started. Remi chided herself for overreacting. *Just listen to the boy.*

Crue shrugged again. "It's not like you did anything wrong," he began. "Things have just gotten really rough at home, and I went looking for you to talk."

"What do you mean by – went looking?"

"I was on the northside of town, so I went to your house."

Remi feigned surprise. "Crue, that's wrong on so many levels. You're a smart young man. This office is where we can talk about your troubles. But not at my home." She thought she saw something change in his eyes. Like a child reprimanded, or a defiant teenager told what to do, his demeanor changed. "Is that understood?"

"Why are you behaving like the rest of them? That's what makes you different. You don't judge, you don't bitch. You're not listening to me like you have all the other times before."

"I'm listening, Crue. I just need you to hear me first. This is where our sessions will take place. Do you want to tell me why things have gotten more difficult at home?"

"My mother slit her wrists. They found her in time, but now she's under serious surveillance around the clock. If she can't drink, she doesn't want to be a part of this world. Nothing means more to her than vodka."

"I'm sorry that your mom is in pain, and you as well," Remi began, carefully. "I know it's easier said than done, but try to see that she doesn't love you any less because she needs alcohol. It's an addiction that's taken over her mind and body. She can't think straight. She wants to, but the parts of her brain that are begging for a drink have clouded all of her emotions. Try to understand that."

"I overheard my dad say to his girlfriend, our very own Miss Pilgreen here in this building," Crue added with a snarky tone, "that he wishes she would have bled to death."

Remi tried not to overreact. She kept her facial expression free of surprise or disgust. "Oh my word. I'm sure he didn't mean it. He's angry with her because she's hurt him in the past."

"Don't defend him. There's no excuse. He never should have said it," Crue stated, and Remi understood. "Things go through my mind all the time, too, but I don't say what I'm thinking."

"Like what?" Remi pushed.

"Nothing," Crue spat back at her, and instantly stood in front of his chair.

"We still have ten minutes, Crue. Sit back down. Please."

"I have to go," he stated as a matter of fact, and he turned his back and walked out of her office. He closed the door so swiftly behind him that it bounced back open after he walked away.

Remi sat at her desk for several minutes after he left. Thinking. And pondering what could have changed. He didn't want to open up to her today. He was not at all like himself. Her mind kept going back to the same thing each time she tried to identify a reason behind his anger toward her. If she had not witnessed him show up at her house, she never would have come to the conclusion she had. But it could be true. His feelings had escalated quickly. That was not unheard of with troubled teens who were attention starved. *Crue had become too attached to her. Obsessed – might be the better word choice.*

Chapter 13

Remi eventually convinced herself that she was overreacting. Crue had a lot to deal with in his young adult life, including the recent scare with his mother making an attempt to take her own life. She kept her thoughts to herself regarding Crue and the fact that he had overstepped a professional boundary when he showed up at her house. She pushed any feeling of panic or uneasiness aside, and she was confident that Crue would be back in her office the following day. If anything, she was his escape the first half of his sixth-hour class.

Crue never showed up. By the second day, Remi stopped in the main office to talk to the attendance secretary.

"Hey Remi, what brings you down to my end today?" Letitia had been in that seat, Remi was told, for the past fifteen years. She was a fixture there. There was never a question which she could not answer or be quick to find a solution to. And everyone was always received with an infectious smile.

"Any excuse to see you, dear," Remi stated, and Letitia's round face blushed.

"You're a good fit here," Letitia complimented Remi in return. "I've heard the kids love you in guidance."

Remi smiled wide before she got to the point of why she was really there. "Those kids feed my soul. One, in particular, concerns me lately though. I stopped in here to check to see if he's been absent from school or just avoiding my sessions." Remi hadn't spotted Crue in the crowded hallways either when she ventured out of her office.

"Who's that?" Letitia asked, obviously ready to play detective for Remi.

"Crue Macke."

Letitia didn't need to plug his name into her computer. She knew. "He's been a no-show for the past two days, and his father doesn't answer our check-in calls." The high school's policy was to call any parent whose child had an unexcused absence.

"That worries me more," Remi stated honestly. "So now what? Does our principal follow up in any way?"

Letitia shook her head and lowered her voice, as the principal's cushy office was directly behind them. "Typically, yes, but Rhonda stepped in, so this has all been swept under the rug." Rhonda, of course, was Miss Pilgreen, who was dating Crue's father and clearly had made no secret of it to anyone.

"What did she say?" Remi asked.

"I'm not sure exactly. All I know is that our administrator allowed her to be Crue's acting parent, so the absences have been excused." Letitia rolled her eyes.

"I see," Remi responded, and she didn't think that was a bad thing. But she was still very concerned about Crue, and now her curiosity had peaked. *What was Rhonda Pilgreen trying to cover up for him?* "When is Miss Pilgreen's planning period?" Remi thought it wouldn't hurt to ask, or stop by her classroom for a little chat.

"Next hour," Letitia winked at her, as Remi patted her on the hand and then walked away as if she had somewhere to be.

ꝏꝏ

Remi knocked twice on the frame of Rhonda Pilgreen's open door. She looked up from the chair behind her desk.

"Remi, hi. Come in."

"I know planning periods are important, so I'll be brief," Remi stated out of courtesy, and with the hope of starting off this conversation on a positive note.

Rhonda waved her in. "You're fine. How are things going for you here?"

"Good. I enjoy my job, and everyone here has been incredibly welcoming."

"Well that's wonderful," Rhonda smiled. It was a smile that could be taken two ways. Sincere or phony. Remi had yet to decide which.

"I don't want to make you uncomfortable," Remi began, "but I have to ask you something regarding a student I've counseled regularly."

"Crue's fine," Rhonda chimed in, without hesitating. She knew why Remi was there.

"Why the need to skip school then?" If there was one thing Remi always did, it was that she laid the facts on the line. If she wanted to know something, she didn't hesitate to ask. And if she was, in turn, asked something, she gave an honest answer. That's what most people liked about her.

"Are you aware of the latest drama with his mother?" *Spoken like a true girlfriend who was not on good terms with the ex-woman in her man's life,* Remi thought.

"If you're referring to her suicide attempt, yes," Remi answered her.

Rhonda nodded. "Crue's having a difficult time with that. He went up to Springfield for a few days. His father checked him into a hotel. He's allowed to see his mother thirty minutes a day."

"So he's alone there?" Remi frowned.

"When he's not with his mother, yes," Rhonda stated, nonchalantly. It was as if she was relieved to have her man to herself while his son was away. Remi was not at all getting a motherly vibe from her. She wondered if she even cared for Crue. He was unstable right now, and probably should not be alone. Remi believed her opinion was fact.

"Has he ever said anything to you about me, or our sessions?" Remi asked.

"Shouldn't that be confidential?" Rhonda all but snapped. Her tone of voice had definitely gone from nice to bitchy. *She was phony,* Remi had now concluded.

"Of course," Remi spoke, "but as professionals in the same working environment, I'm asking if I have reason to be concerned about anything at all. Anything that you might have an inside glance of, given the fact that you are with his father."

With was a safe word. *Fucking* was inappropriate. Remi suppressed a giggle.

"He's a good kid," Rhonda answered, vaguely.

Remi stood there, in front of her desk, waiting for her to say more. To elaborate even just a little bit to confirm her theory that Crue's recent actions were simply off and had raised a red flag. But Rhonda Pilgreen was finished talking.

"Okay then, thank you for sharing with me where Crue's been," Remi wanted to roll her eyes at herself. She was being just as phony.

"Absolutely."

And that concluded their chit chat.

Remi left, and Rhonda sunk back into her chair. She promised Crue's father that she would protect his son. Her romantic relationship was at stake. She hadn't had a man, long-term, in her life for far too long. She would keep to herself the creepy and alarming fact that she found a shrine of photographs —solely of Remi—taped to the inside of Crue's bedroom closet door. Crue's father brushed it off as his son was just a horny teenager with a crush on his counselor. Rhonda had stared long and hard at the photographs. One was the newspaper clipping from the O'Fallon Progress Newspaper, the article that welcomed the new hires for the current school year and Remi was featured. All of the other photographs were taken of Remi in her office, she assumed with Crue's cell phone. Clearly unbeknownst to Remi. This felt wrong on so many levels, Rhonda mused, but she wasn't about to lose the new man in her life. Not for anyone.

Chapter 14

This time Kate walked Livy inside Tucker's house when it was again his turn to have her for a couple nights. As had already become a routine, Livy carried with her a backpack and a few baby dolls. Tucker picked her up and swung her around in circles in the middle of the living room as Kate stood back and smiled. *That little girl and her daddy. Or maybe, it was that daddy and his little girl.* They adored each other. Sometimes Kate judged herself and questioned her own morals. She was the cause that snatched that constant away from the two of them, forcing them to make the most of their stolen moments divvied up into a couple days at a time.

Livy darted into her bedroom to gather all of her baby dolls together as a family, she stated, and Tucker took a moment to really think about what she had said. *Even the baby dolls were living the broken family life between two homes.*

"Did she just imply what I think she did?" Tucker asked Kate, as she had picked up on that, too.

"I think so, but she didn't seem sad about it. I mean, she gets it. Liv is smart. She knows not everyone lives the same type of life. We are not cookie cutter human beings with perfect lives." Kate was proud of her own analogy.

"Right," Tucker stated. "She is smart enough to deal with this, that's for sure." He did want to question how he thought Kate had sought after and found *the perfect life. Hadn't she?* He refrained from asking.

"I should go," Kate said, but she wanted to say goodbye to Livy first. It wasn't her house anymore to waltz down the hallway in search of her child. She was about to call out her name instead, and Tucker stopped her.

"Wait, before you head out, I have something for you." He turned his back and walked in the direction of the kitchen. For a moment, Kate wondered what he had for her. Tucker was a thoughtful man. She missed some of those little things in her life. She could have cursed herself for having these thoughts in this house. *She was not a bad person for choosing a different path for herself. Livy was adjusting. Tucker had romantically moved on with another woman – although Kate didn't see that lasting long-term.*

Tucker looked expressionless when he walked back into the living room where Kate was waiting. It wasn't easy to sign off, to end his marriage. He never wanted that. Kate did. But he believed it was much easier to move on and to live his life now that Remi was a part of it. Remi was not Kate. And Kate certainly was not her. But he had considered himself a fortunate man to have loved twice in his life. Two very different women had touched his heart. One broke it, and the other now played a part in mending it.

When Kate realized what Tucker was holding in his hand, she felt a lump rise in her throat. She initially imagined having to ask him twice or three times to hand over the signed divorce papers. And here he was willingly offering them to her, signed, and ready to finalize the end of Tucker and Kate Brandt. And the ring on her finger was the promise that she would one day be Kate Ratchford.

"Here you go," he said, reaching out to her with their divorce agreement in his hand. Kate hesitated to reach back, but when she finally did with her left hand, her diamond ring caught the sunlight peering through the front picture window, and that in turn grabbed Tucker's attention.

"Looks like you need to file these papers soon," Tucker motioned his eyes on her ring.

"Yeah," Kate replied, nervously twisting the ring with the fingers on her opposite hand. "Riley asked me to marry him."

"Good," he spoke in no uncertain terms and with very little emotion in his voice or on his face.

"Good?" Kate questioned him, feeling offended nonetheless. She chided herself for it, but she actually had liked knowing that Tucker still loved her, and pined for her.

"He's following through. He wants a life with you. I didn't want to see you end up with a broken heart."

Thoughtful Tucker.

"I never wanted that for you either, to hurt you, I mean." Kate was trying to find the right words to say to keep this moment from becoming too awkward between them. Tucker stayed silent, because dammit she had hurt him badly. He'd never felt an emotional pain like it in his life. "I want you to be happy, too," Kate added.

"I am," he was quick to respond. "I don't have to explain to you how fast you can give your heart to someone else when the right person comes along." Kate still wondered if she had truly given Riley her heart. And it actually hurt her to hear that Tucker was completely certain Remi had his.

Kate only nodded. This time it was her turn to believe it was best to stay silent. There were too many questions unanswered in her mind and heart now. More than before. "I need to say goodbye to Liv," she swayed their conversation off its path.

Tucker called out to Livy. When she ran into the living room, still holding one of the baby dolls she brought from her other house, Kate freed her hands of the papers when she placed them on the coffee table near her.

They hugged, kissed, and did their goodbye-for-now ritual. This time it was Tucker, who stood back and watched the two of them. *That girl and her mommy. Everyone had faults, but this woman, the mother of his child, was a good mother.*

"Call me if you need me," Tucker heard Kate say, as Livy pulled him by the hand to go play in her room.

It wasn't until much later in the evening when Tucker and Livy settled down in the living room to watch a Disney movie that Tucker noticed the divorce papers left on the coffee table. *Kate had forgotten to take them along.* He thought she was in a hurry to end their marriage. Tucker knew how badly Kate wanted to move on with her life. Or so he thought.

ᴔᴔ

Remi was expecting him. Tucker had spent a couple days with Livy, and during that time Remi had declined two of his offers to join them. She thought it was too soon for Livy to see them together, acting like a couple, and she had too much weighing on her mind and needed the time alone to think. An entire week had gone by and Crue still had not returned to school. No one seemed to have any concerns except for Remi. She, after all, was the one Crue was upset with when he left. The way he stormed out of the guidance office was still a vivid image. He acted like a man jilted. Remi did not have a good vibe about this now. Despite what her colleague had said. She wasn't so sure she should trust Rhonda Pilgreen anyway. Crue's words still rang in her ears.

Why are you behaving like the rest of them? That's what makes you different. You don't judge, you don't bitch. You're not listening to me like you have all the other times before.

Had she let him down? She knew she had to be careful if he walked back into her office upon his return to school. Remi still wanted to help him. She hoped to regain his trust. But this time, she was aware that Crue's state of mind was not as mature and stable as he wanted her to perceive.

She opened her front door to Tucker. The sight of him warmed her heart, and other places. They were both still in their work clothes. "Hi," he said to her first and she stepped back for him to come inside.

"Hi there," Remi smiled. She missed him. She didn't like how lonely she felt without him. But to say those words to him was something she held back on. It's who she was now. But Tucker did have a way of reaching beyond her barriers.

"I missed you," he said it first, and she could have foreseen that he would.

"Yeah?" she asked, grinning at him. There was still too much physical space between them. They had not yet touched. Or kissed. "I thought it was best for you to have your daddy time with Livy."

Tucker nodded. "I know it. There will be time for the three of us to hang out together. She and I had a good couple of days again. I miss her already."

"I wish it didn't have to be that way for you," Remi stated, honestly.

"Me too," he agreed, "but she is adjusting well, so for that I'm grateful. Kate is a good mother. She just ended up not being the most loyal wife." Tucker smirked.

"People have issues with loyalty," Remi also spoke from experience. And she was not sure if she would ever understand why. All she ever wanted her entire life thus far was for someone to stay. To want to stay and be with her.

"Rem," Tucker spoke, and she liked how he shortened her name. It was the first time he had done that. "I don't." She knew he was referring to having issues with loyalty. "If you're in my life, you have my allegiance, my faithfulness, and my devotion. It's who I am."

"I believe you," she smiled at him. Goodness. She had been looking for someone like him for her whole life. And the moment she had stopped, and basically had thrown up her hands and given up, there he was.

"Good," he said, and he wanted to step closer to her and take her into his arms. But, with Remi, Tucker always chose to wait for her cue. Today, she seemed more distant again. He blamed that on their time apart. He didn't like being away from her. He didn't want to sift through the initial awkwardness again with her.

"You know, it's my turn to cook for you. Would you like to stay for dinner?" Remi asked him, and he liked the fleeting mischievous look he caught in her eyes.

"I was waiting for you to ask," he chuckled. "Can I help in the kitchen?"

"Sure," she told him, "but I need to get out of these clothes first." For a split second, Tucker genuinely thought Remi only wanted to change into something more comfortable for the evening. Women did that sort of thing. But then she asked him for help with unzipping the back of her dress.

∞∞

The time got away from them, and their plans to cook dinner had to be altered once they got out of bed and opted to order a pizza. Tucker was back in his jeans with his Rix Hardware polo shirt untucked. He was barefoot and standing in her bedroom as Remi threw on a pair of plaid pajama pants and a white t-shirt.

"You really are sexy in anything," he told her.

"Awe well aren't you the sweetest, or should I say the horniest?"

"I'll take that," he chuckled, stepping toward her, and she reached out her arm and held up her hand.

"Nope. Stop. No more. We have to eat." She was laughing while she spoke and Tucker pinched her buttock before he ran from her bedroom with her following. Their relationship was fun. That's what it came down to. They could talk, they could fall into bed with just one look, and they effortlessly could laugh at anything. They were young enough yet to begin again and fall in love, but neither one of them had confessed those feelings to the other yet. Tucker was ready, Remi was not. He knew that.

Remi squealed when Tucker turned around abruptly as they were running, and she fell into him. He kissed her hard on the mouth and she no doubt responded. And then the doorbell rang.

They parted quickly from each other, and Remi spoke in a soft tone of voice. "It's the pizza guy already. I need to grab my purse from the kitchen."

"I got it," Tucker declared as he reached behind him for his wallet in his back pocket.

"No, no, no! I owe you something for the mailbox."

"Oh you've paid that debt in full, honey," Tucker winked at her, and she laughed out loud at what he implied.

He waved a twenty-dollar-bill into the air and she snatched it from him before she went to the door. Remi swung it open, still grinning from Tucker's implication. But that smile faded the moment she saw Crue standing on her front porch.

Chapter 15

"Crue?" She wanted to say, *didn't I make myself clear about this?* But he spoke first.

"Before you object, please, it's been a difficult week," he began to plea, and Remi thought how she had never seen him this way before. *Vulnerable.*

And then she watched him look past her as Tucker walked up and stood close behind her. Crue clearly was not the pizza delivery guy.

"Hello," Tucker greeted Crue in his polite salesman voice. And then he looked at Remi as if to say, *who's this?*

Crue's eyes widened. "I didn't know you, um, weren't by yourself. You're attached?" Those words alone confirmed what Remi recently began to fear. Crue thought of her as more than just his counselor.

"That's personal," Remi told him in the most polite, professional way possible. "I'll see you on Monday in my office." She meant it. This had to be the last time that he overstepped. "That's where I'm able to counsel you."

Crue only stared back at her. Tucker looked confused and he stayed quiet. Remi could hold her own. But the kid wasn't leaving. Remi momentarily worried that she had been too harsh. Troubled teens often resorted to drastic measures. But this, his actions alone, felt drastic. She wanted to avoid trouble with this young man. She had to.

"I'll go," he finally said. "I want to talk to you...but it can wait until we're alone." Crue had the audacity to stare at Tucker for a moment before he coyly smiled at Remi and finally turned and walked to his blue coup once again parked on her driveway.

Remi swiftly closed the door behind her and made the quick motion to turn the deadbolt. Tucker spun her around by the shoulders. He could see the panic in her eyes and now she was trembling.

"What the hell just happened? He's one of your students?"

Remi quickly regained her composure, led him over to the sofa, and explained that tonight was not his first attempt to pay her a visit in the privacy of her own home. She told him everything, breaking the confidentiality code and all. She trusted Tucker. The only thing she could not do was call the police as he strongly suggested.

"He's a kid, Tucker. And besides, I can't draw attention to this. It could cost me my job if the wrong rumor got started."

"What about your safety?" Tucker had a valid point.

"Can we compromise? I'll go to my principal tomorrow. I'll tell him that Crue overstepped." Remi wasn't entirely sure that she wanted to go that far.

"Okay, but I don't like this. Not one bit. Did you see how that kid eyed me? I was not a part of his plan tonight. He wants to get you alone, Remi. He wants you all to himself. I saw the way he looked at you. That's obsessive behavior."

Remi covered her mouth with her hand and nodded. She was scared. "I've been afraid of that being the truth."

"You should have told me," Tucker's voice was gentle but firm.

"You've been busy with Livy, and this isn't your problem. It's mine. I don't burden people."

Tucker took both of her hands in his. "First of all, I am here for you anytime, no matter what I'm doing or who I'm with. And even more significant," Tucker inhaled a slow deep breath, "you need to get past feeling like a burden to me. Lean on me. Turn to me. I want to be able to do all the same with you. It's what people do when they love each other."

Remi fought the tears that wanted to well up behind her eyes. "We do, don't we?" she spoke in barely a whisper. *They loved each other.*

"Yeah," he chuckled, "we do." But before he could pull her into his arms, the doorbell rang again. Remi immediately jumped. "It's the pizza," Tucker reassured her as he got up from the sofa. He already made the decision to stay the night with Remi. She was his to protect now.

ꝏꝏ

The moment Riley told Kate that they needed to talk, she saw a red flag. His words, *we need to talk*, were a warning of some sort. Of a problem that lie ahead. The last time Riley wanted to have a heart-to-heart discussion with her, he had bought a-half-of-a-million-dollar house in the same city she lived in. He wanted her to leave her husband —and life as she knew it— to be with him. So, his words, *we need to talk,* had Kate's attention.

He chose her office to talk. Not at the home they shared. Kate wondered if it was because Livy was almost always there with them. And when she was, it was as if Riley let the two of them do their thing, and he did his. Kate told herself that would change once they were married and officially became a family.

"My brother called," he began. Kate knew Riley's history with his older brother. The two of them had worked for the same law firm in San Diego. They were too competitive, too hurtful, and just never got along. A petty disagreement was what had led Riley to quit the firm there and make the move to St. Louis to another law firm. And now Kate assumed his brother had reached out. *But what did a likely olive branch have to do with her? With them?*

"He quit the firm, too," Riley stated. "He's branching out on his own. He bought office space in one of the most prominent skyscrapers in the business district downtown San Diego. It's prized space." Kate took note of how Riley always described everything as being the best and brightest. Not that she complained. She just noticed. The Ratchford boys came from money. "And he wants me to partner with him. Ratchford Law. It's been a dream of ours, really."

"Really?" Kate repeated in a snarky tone. "I thought the two of you all but hated each other? If you don't get along, how will you run a law firm?"

Riley chuckled a bit. "Yeah, that's just who we are. We can put everything else aside for business."

"In San Diego?" Kate was confused and needed clarification quickly.

"Yeah, back home." Kate noticed his classy black suit, two shades of gray swirled together were the color of his tie, and those shiny black loafers. His blond hair with side-swept bangs was almost white. Like hers. She too wore a black business suit – with a short skirt and black high heels. They were a striking pair.

"It's home for you," she stated. Her home was in the Midwest – with Livy.

"For us," he clarified. "We can get married and start our life together in California. How amazing will that be for you, having lived in the same place all of your life!"

Her forehead lines, that she considered Botox injections for, were creased. She grimaced before she spoke. Her facial expression objected before she could verbally form the words. "My life is here. Livy's life is here. Her father is rooted here." It was Riley's turn to scowl. Her ex-husband should not be a part of the equation, or this decision. Tucker, despite how he had never met the man, unnerved him.

"Tucker Brandt isn't your concern. We, the two of us with Livy, are going to be a family."

"He's her father, he has rights. We share custody, and what's going to happen if I'm halfway across the country with our daughter?"

"I thought of that," Riley noted, "and it's all figured out. I bought a private jet. We can get her back and forth on the days that Tucker is scheduled to have her. It's the perfect solution." *He had already bought a jet. Problem solved. Kate was not even included in that decision.*

"And you think I can just put my little girl on an aircraft twice a week?" If Kate had not opened her eyes to the fact before, she did now. *Riley had no idea how to be a parent. He was far from capable of being loving and protective. Even with Kate.* And that was another thing it had taken her entirely too long to grasp.

"You can go back and forth with her until she's comfortable," Riley suggested as if they were just taking a car ride to the next town.

Kate rolled her eyes. "What about our brand-new house? My career?"

"Easily replaced," he stated.

"And me?" she asked him. "Am I easily replaceable?"

"Of course not," Riley answered, and for a moment Kate recognized the fleeting panic in his eyes. It had never occurred to him that Kate would reject his new plan for them. "I love you. We are meant for each other. We both grasped that from the moment we met. Look at all we've been through to be together."

"We? Don't you mean me, and my child? I left my marriage, and uprooted Livy from her family life. You've made no sacrifices that have come even close to what we have. And now you want to move back to your home, and you're asking us to give up more? I can't. No. Absolutely not."

"The house is going on the market tomorrow. I have a week to get back to San Diego. I have a business to help launch there." Everything Riley stated was all about him.

"Sounds like you have a lot to do then," Kate spoke. Her voice was strong, but she was breaking inside. She had made a royal mistake. And it was not just her life she had gambled with – but Livy's, and Tucker's too.

"Take some time to process this," Riley told her, not entirely believing she had made her final decision. And certainly not accepting that they were over. He knew Kate's type. Her makeup was like his. Money trumped everything in the end.

"My daughter comes first. There. I've processed all I need to." Kate glared at him. She was stronger than she felt, she reminded herself. Despite the fact that she was about to be without a fiancé and the big dreams she had of living the perfect life with him. She sacrificed so much for nothing. For it to end this way for her. Divorced. And homeless.

Riley reached out. He held onto her arm too tightly. He pulled her toward him. "You're giving up everything I can offer you? For what? Come with me for it all. Just say yes. Come on, Kate. Where's the woman who takes risks and relishes in the feeling? I can offer you the world. You know that."

"I know," Kate responded. He let go of her arm, and she placed both of her open palms on his chest. "But that's not enough." Even in heels, she had to stand on her tip toes to reach him. She lightly pressed her lips to his. And she closed her eyes for a moment. When she forced herself to back away, she said to him, "Goodbye, Riley."

He tried to object. He had more to say. *"They could live in a bigger house, drive fancier-yet vehicles. Anything she wanted. Their life together could be in California for chrissakes!"*

But Kate kept her back to him as she walked out of her office and closed the door between them.

Chapter 16

While at Rix Hardware, Tucker received a phone call from Kate. "I know I've caught you in the middle of work, but can you get away for awhile and meet me at the house?"

"What's wrong? Is it Livy?" Their little girl was the only connection they had left. Why else would Kate want to meet with him? Their divorce was processing. It was unreal to him how she wanted to talk and expected him to listen to, or understand whatever it was she had to say. For months on end, Tucker had tried to get her to listen to him and to grasp that giving up and leaving was not the answer. *They had a good life together.*

"She's fine. She's in school. I'm on my way from St. Louis." Kate pressed her cell phone to her ear and heard static as she drove her SUV across the Poplar Street Bridge. "I can stop by the store, but I really don't want any interruptions."

Tucker was even more confused, or maybe just irked because he had work to do. "I'll leave here soon," he said, and then he ended their call.

ꝏꝏ

Kate was on the driveway when Tucker pulled up. He parked behind her vehicle, and got out to find her still sitting inside of it. She stepped out when he reached her driver's side door. She stood there, opposite Tucker, in her dark, professionally low-cut business suit and high heels. They clashed with each other as Tucker was in jeans, work boots, and his standard Rix polo shirt. They were so different from each other in many ways. But opposites sometimes attract, and for sure they had. He had dark hair. She was blonde. Not a natural blonde, but a striking salon-made blonde nonetheless. She was rail thin, he was thick. She sought the finer things in life, and he was a simple man.

"Thank you for coming," she said to him, "I mean, thanks for meeting me on short notice."

Tucker nodded. "Let's go inside." Fall temperatures had settled in the air, and while the chill was inviting, neither one of them wanted to stand out there for too long. Tucker hoped, however, that this impromptu meeting wouldn't take too much time. For a moment, he glanced behind him at Remi's house. She was at work, and he knew she typically took her lunch break at the high school. It's not that he was concerned about Remi seeing Kate at his house in the middle of the day, but he did suddenly feel uncomfortable with the thought. He was committed to Remi now. He didn't owe Kate the time of day, or anything at all if it did not pertain to Livy. But, yet, here he was granting her request to be there.

Kate followed him inside the front door. They both momentarily stood in the living room. The sun coming through the front window blinds lit up the entire area. *The white leather sectional she bought without Tucker's consent. The cherry-wood furniture she had to have.* That room was still all her, but it was not hers to own anymore. She left everything behind when

Riley completely furnished their brand-new house. All she and Livy had packed up and brought with them were clothes – and toys.

"So, what is it? What's going on?" Tucker kept standing. Kate knew he did not want to make himself comfortable as she had made him feel uneasy. He had gone from sad and miserable without her to beside-himself-happy with someone else already. Kate was now only his ex-wife and mother of his child. She could no longer see love in his eyes, and the timing of everything in her life right now was beyond unfortunate. Kate had undoubtedly screwed up.

Kate walked over to one end of the sectional and sat down on the edge of it. She kept both of her heels planted on the hardwood floor, her bare knees pressed closely together. She smoothed the top of her skirt with the open palms of her hands. "I know that I hurt you," she began, *because where else could she possibly begin?* "And I'm sorry for that." Tucker stayed quiet, but he wondered why she was apologizing now. *What happened to the suck-it-up-and-move-on, woman?* "I made some rash decisions based on wealth and prestige, and all that both could offer. I've always been a small-town girl with big dreams."

"Yet the dreamer loves this cozy town," Tucker said, because he knew her well. While the City of O'Fallon had tripled its size over the course of both Kate and Tucker's lives, it still meant so much to both of them. That hometown-feel of it had not gotten lost in its tremendous growth and prosperity. Kate smiled at him. He knew her well. He understood her best.

"You're right," she completely agreed with him, and then she got to the point of why she was there. "I screwed up, Tucker. I did what every fool does. I gambled everything on the grass being greener somewhere else." Tucker looked at her left hand.

She still wore *Riley's* ridiculously large diamond ring. "Riley is putting our new house on the market. He's moving back to San Diego to start up his own law firm. It was an offer from his brother that apparently was too wonderful to refuse. He already purchased a private jet with the sole purpose of getting Livy back and forth to you."

With every word she spoke, Tucker's shock deepened. *What in the actual fuck?* It was as if the words, his reaction to this insanity, were frozen in his mind and would not roll off his tongue. There was no possible way he was going to allow her, them, to take his daughter that far away from him. Nor, to put Livy in harm's way thousands of feet up in the air on a regular basis. *Kids rode bikes, not flew all over creation on private jets.*

Tucker finally found his voice. "Tell me you're joking, because there is no way in hell I will allow it." Kate knew him well. She expected this reaction. And he was about to discover that she wholeheartedly agreed with him. Enough to walk away from everything she thought she wanted. *All that she could have had.*

"It's no joke. It's reality. Riley's idea of reality."

"Yeah?" Tucker spat at her, while she remained calm and seated on the sectional, and he paced the floor in front of her. "And just where is Riley? He's never shown his face around me, has he? And why is that, Kate? Because he's a coward, that's why. He's bold enough to take another man's family from him, but not to face him. I'm him, Kate. And he already took my wife, so like hell if I am going to stand back and allow that SOB to take my daughter!" There was something comforting about the way Tucker claimed her. Kate inhaled a deep breath through her nostrils, and hoped to God she could reach him with the rest of what she had to share.

"You're not going to meet Riley," Kate spoke seriously. "I'm leaving him. Livy and I are moving out of his house. He can make the move to California without us. That life, that far away, was not what I had envisioned with him. I would never take Livy from you. You know that."

Tucker breathed a loud sigh of relief. His emotions were in overdrive. The thought of Livy living in California was too much. It was hard enough that she lived across town from him. His thoughts reeled, and then it suddenly crossed his mind – *where would the two of them live now?* Tucker wanted to thank Kate, but that just felt too damn awkward. She was going to confuse Livy yet again. She brought a man into her life, who was supposed to play the part of her stepfather, and now he was going to be gone.

"I don't know what to think anymore," he told her. "You let me down in the worst way. You've put Livy through some big changes in her life already. I thought you had what you wanted. And now just like that you're done? You're leaving Mr. Almighty and where, just exactly where, are you going next?" Tucker was angry. He was relieved that Livy was not going to be carted off halfway across the country. But still, this news hurt. Kate had played with fire and they all had ended up burned.

"You make it sound as if you're unhappy with my decision not to take Livy and move with him to California?" Kate sounded snarky.

"You know better than that," Tucker reacted.

She nodded her head. "Yes, I do. And I know you're upset with me for being so foolish. I'm angry at myself, too, believe me."

"Well that doesn't make it all better, or suddenly acceptable."

"I agree," Kate told him.

"So now what? What now?" Tucker repeated himself.

"I'm moving out of Riley's house, and Livy and I will find another place here in O'Fallon. It might be temporary until we find a house that fits. I might need you to keep her for a few unplanned days while I figure things out for us."

Tucker did not nod or comply in any way, but that wasn't necessary as he would always be there for his daughter. "I just don't believe this," he admitted, shaking his head at her as if she was a child and he was the responsible all-knowing parent.

The last thing Kate needed was to be reprimanded, or to hear *I told you so.* She felt teary just sitting there now. She also felt vulnerable. To life. To him. "Tucker?"

She spoke his name. She had his attention. "What?"

"Riley filed our divorce agreement, but I'm not sure it's been finalized yet." Those words, from her, tore him apart. *She was his first true love. His wife of five years. The mother of his little girl.* If certain fate-like things had not happened to him since she walked out, if this exact moment was in another time and another place, he may have been hopeful or possibly overjoyed. But that was then and this was now. Tucker had moved on with his life. He had managed to close off his heart to her, his past, and open it to Remi, his future. He was in love with Remi Jasper. Not Kate. Not anymore.

"And what exactly do you mean by that?" Tucker asked her, and at this moment Kate was unsure of how to read him. *Was he hopeful? Or was she too late?* She wasn't going to allow herself to feel defeated just yet.

"I don't want a divorce," she responded, not taking her eyes off him. *He was once hers. He could be again.*

"Kate," it was his turn to speak her name with a long pause after. "I couldn't measure up to what you thought you wanted. You left me for a better man, in your mind and heart. To be made to feel that way takes something away from a man. I am many things, but I am no one's second best."

Kate covered her mouth with her hand. She choked on a sob before she spoke to him again. "I deserved that," she said, "but second chances are sometimes a way to make what you once had stronger and better than it ever was."

"No. That's not going to be the case for us," Tucker replied adamantly. "Look, I don't want to hurt you. I sure as hell do not want to inflict the same kind of pain on you that you did me. Not once did you flinch when you shoved your true feelings and your new plans down my throat. All there is to say is what you already know. I am with Remi now because I want to be. I have no intention of halting our divorce agreement."

Kate allowed the tears to freefall from her eyes and onto her face. Her makeup wasn't so flawless anymore. Her mascara smeared. This was exactly what it felt like to be on the receiving end of heartache. Tucker really was never second best in her heart. She had learned that truth in the most painful way.

Chapter 17

Remi was unable to catch the high school principal in the building before the school day began. She sent him a personal email, requesting to meet as soon as his schedule allowed. She remembered that life with Sam and how his calendar could be hectic and demanding at times at the helm of a high school. She assumed her boss and Principal Mike Kinsall would have time for her soon.

As it turned out, Remi had gone through almost the entire school day without an email response, nor had she spotted her boss in the crowded hallways. It was now five minutes prior to the sixth hour. She expected Crue to show up. And suddenly she wished she had a flask of vodka hidden in her desk drawer. *Relax Remi. You're the adult here. Be professional. Get a grip.*

He was on time.

Remi sat behind her desk, readily punching keys on her laptop. It was busy work to calm her nerves.

"Miss Jasper?" Crue wanted her attention from the doorway. She left the door open on purpose, and while she typically asked her students to close it once they stepped inside, today she would have been more comfortable with it wide open. *Or taken completely off the hinges.*

"Come on in, Crue." Remi spoke, trying to sound as normal as possible, as she watched him close the door behind him.

He sat down in silence, but he knew the rules in that office. Students had to speak first. "Can we get the awkward out of the way first?" he asked her, and Remi was not surprised by his directness. It's who he was. She waited for him to continue. "I crossed the line. I know it, and I also know you are upset with me because of it. It will not happen again," he added, and Remi wondered if she should even attempt to believe him. After all, he had come to her house and broken the rules twice. Crue didn't know she had seen him the first time.

"Okay," was all Remi replied.

"I went to see my mother in Springfield. My dad put me up in a hotel for a few days."

"How did your visit with her go?" Remi asked, both concerned and curious because previously at her house Crue had mentioned it being the end of a difficult week.

"I actually had three visits with her. One a day for thirty minutes at a time," Crue explained. "We were given a private room to talk. I just want my mom back, you know? The one pre-booze who could think straight, and cared about me."

"I'm sure your mother cares," Remi spoke in defense of a woman she had not even known. But, in theory, all mothers were supposed to care.

"I'm not as confident," Crue stated. "She was distant. I can have meaningless small talk with my neighbor, or my dad's girlfriend for that matter." Remi wanted to roll her eyes. She was not a fan of Miss Pilgreen. "By day three, she told me that it would be best if I didn't come there anymore. She wants to get better first. I asked her if we could talk on the phone, and she blew me off, making an excuse about time restraints or something. She's abandoned me, that's the bottom line." Crue sunk lower in his chair, and fidgeted with the distressed denim on his torn knee. She noticed the curls all over his head were overgrown.

"I'm sorry," Remi began. She kicked into professional gear, but personally she felt his pain. She could relate, as her own father had left her. "Your mother is troubled. She's struggling to remain sober, and her attempt to take her own life was a desperate cry for help."

"I know that, that's why I went to her. She didn't seem to care." Crue stared straight ahead at Remi, waiting, as if she had the magic answer to bring him out of the slump his mother had shoved him down into.

Remi opted to switch gears. The direction of telling him that *his mother still cared, she just had an odd way of expressing it,* was not working. "I was eleven years old when my father abandoned me." Crue's expression changed. "My parents divorced, and he never held up his end of the bargain to be a parent to me. He vanished from my life, and I have not seen or heard from him since."

"I'm sorry for that," Crue spoke, as if he was trying to comfort her over something she appeared to long have gotten over. "Have you ever tried to find him?"

Remi paused. This was getting personal, and she wondered if that was wise. *Given all things considered with this young man.* "No. I'm quite content without him in my life. If someone doesn't want me, I am not going to chase them or beg them. I have my morals and my pride." Her final statement was indirectly meant for Crue. If he had any inappropriate feelings for her, he needed to get them in check before he made a complete fool of himself.

Crue smiled, and Remi could not quite read the meaning behind his expression, or precisely what he was thinking. "There's common ground between us," he spoke, and Remi immediately wanted to call him out as being out of bounds. "You get me. And that's why I am drawn to you. I want to be in here every sixth period, and yes I was prompted to visit your home, to see you in your element. You could do better than that hardware guy though."

"Enough!" Remi snapped, and stood up from behind her desk. She stood so abruptly that her chair on wheels rolled back and bounced off the wall. "It's time for you to go. I will not tolerate this behavior from you. Today was your second chance, and you blew it. I will notify Miss Pilgreen that you will be returning to her class for the full class period beginning tomorrow." As the Director of Guidance, she would also hand over this student to a new counselor. All of this was going to be brought to the attention of her building principal. Remi was finished with Crue.

He never made any attempt to move from his chair. He was strangely calm, and Remi tried to conceal the fact that she was not. Her hands were trembling.

"You can go now," she told him, firmly. And she stared at him. She was scared out of her mind that this young man was more dangerous than anyone believed, namely her from the very beginning.

Finally, Crue stood. And he smiled. It was one Remi saw as more of creepy smirk. And then he turned and walked out of her office, leaving the door wide open this time.

ꝏꝏ

Tucker was so lost in thought that he never heard the first knock on his front door. Remi knocked harder the second time. The glass storm door separated her from going inside, and when Tucker saw her through it from across the room, he waved her in.

"You don't have to knock," he told her with a welcomed smile. He needed her there right now.

"You still ring my bell," she quipped.

"Well I won't again," he chuckled, as she made her way over to him. He was seated on the sofa and she plopped down close beside him. He kissed her first. She responded.

"You first," she said to him when they parted lips.

"What?" he asked, slightly confused.

"The look on your face tells me that your day just might have been as crazy as mine. Tell me about it, so it will take my mind off things."

"You're good," he complimented her. "One look and you've got me all figured out."

"You're an easy read," she teased him, and he squeezed her bare knee. She was still wearing a sapphire blue sweater dress from her work day.

"I'm just plain easy. Why don't you take me to bed so neither of us have to do any talking," he suggested, and Remi giggled.

"Oh we'll get there," she spoke and laughed out loud. "Tell me what's bothering you."

"I want to know about that crazy kid first. I got your text that you are no longer going to counsel him. So, your talk with the principal did some good?"

"Not exactly," Remi admitted. "My boss was out of the building today, and I went ahead with my session with Crue. It was going well, or so I thought, until he crossed the line. He insinuates things, he oversteps. I told him he's done seeing me for counseling. His reaction was just creepy. Tomorrow I hope something more will get done regarding him. I think the staff needs to be on guard. He's not in a good frame of mind."

"I want you to be safe, and keep your doors locked at all times," Tucker told her.

"I will," she nodded her head. "I was hoping you would stay with me again." Remi didn't ask for favors like this, and Tucker was not about to disappoint her.

"You can stay here," he stated.

"Really? Okay, for the sake of something different," she implied, even though they had been in his bed before. Just not as much as hers, and not yet overnight.

"There's something you need to know first." Tucker turned serious. The bothersome look she saw before resurfaced.

"Livy will be here, and she's going to stay with me for a few days."

"I didn't know she was due back so soon. No, really, Tucker, I will be fine. I do not need to impose. I can't stay when she's living here. We've talked about this, it's too soon." Remi realized she needed to put on her big girl panties and take care of herself. She could handle locking her own doors and going to bed.

"I disagree. I think it's time that we explain to her in the simplest terms possible that you are in my life now." Tucker was adamant, and Remi did like the idea of being in his life.

"We don't have to rush this," Remi pressed.

"I'm not. Let's just be together."

"Okay," Remi agreed, because that's what she wanted as well. But Livy was his child, and anything pertaining to her was his decision. "Is something going on with Kate?" Remi assumed she was going away on an adventure with her new love. Tucker had already told her they were now engaged.

"She came to see me today," Tucker began. "The cliff notes version of her mess is that her fiancé has taken a job offer back where he's from, in San Diego. He wanted to move Kate and Livy with him, and start their new life there."

"They can't do that. They can't take her that far away from you. Tucker, you have rights."

"I do, and they are not moving away with Livy."

Remi's eyes instantly widened. "Wait… is Kate going with him and leaving Livy here?"

"No," Tucker was quick to respond. "She's a better mother than that. She broke off her engagement and entire relationship with him actually."

Remi felt her heartbeat quicken. *What did this mean? Lives were again about to change. And they were all going to be affected. Even her.*

"I can read the expressions on your face, too, you know?" Tucker told her. "Stop. There's no need to worry about us. You know where we stand. You know how I feel."

"What if she begs for your forgiveness and comes back here wanting to be a family with you and Livy again?" Remi knew Kate's type. She was impressionable. She got what she wanted. Remi was angry just thinking that Kate could return and attempt to make Tucker feel as if he was good enough for her again. Remi wasn't a fool. She knew that Tucker once deeply loved her. And he was not the one who wanted to see an end to their marriage.

"She already has." Tucker was not going to keep any secrets from Remi. He wanted to be completely honest and for her to know that Kate suggested putting a stop to the divorce proceedings if they had not gone through yet. He also wanted her to know that after a single phone call to the St. Louis City Courthouse, he was informed that he and Kate were in fact already divorced.

Remi stood up, and began to pace the floor in front of Tucker. He smiled a little because they were alike in that way. "I can't believe this. When I allowed you into my world, and gave myself permission to fall for you, I completely trusted that Kate was out of the picture, gone from your life – other than with anything that concerned Livy."

"You were not misled," Tucker told her, as he stood up to meet her in the middle of the floor. "I wasn't either for that matter. Kate wanted out. And now Kate wants back in. But, so what?"

Remi swallowed hard the lump in her throat. No one in her life ever stayed. She believed with all her heart though that it was going to be different with Tucker. She had been gullible enough to trust that he was the one she could count on for the rest of forever. Even though it was very soon to see forever with him, she could envision it.

"Rem..." She loved when he shortened her name. She loved everything about him. "I told Kate, I mean it, I set her straight. She knows that I want to be with you."

"You have no idea how that makes me feel to know that," Remi stated, still fighting the urge to fall apart. "But Tucker, what's happened here and now, makes me a homewrecker." She cleared her throat when her voice cracked. "I'm standing in the way of Livy's parents getting back together."

Tucker took both of his hands and placed them, opened palmed, on each side of her face. And he looked directly into her eyes. "I do not want Kate anymore. She's my past, and you are my future. Don't be freaked out and scared away by my saying that so soon, please. It's just how I feel, Rem." Her heart was fulfilled and ached at the very same time, and she wanted more than anything to fall into him. "I love you so much," he told her.

She loved him, too. But she couldn't say it. Especially not now.

"I'm not freaking out," she lied. "I know how you feel." She never said she loved him back though. "I just think you need to be sure. Be certain of what kind of life you want for Livy." Remi backed away from his touch.

"No. No, come on, Remi. Don't do this. Stay. Work through this with me. Just be with me. It's effortless between us, you know that. You feel it, too."

She did feel it, and that's what made walking away so terribly difficult for her. Tucker pulled her into his arms. He used force, out of his desperation to love her and to save the two of them, and Remi responded. He embraced her, and she held onto him for dear life. She never cried. She was stronger than that, she repeatedly told herself. And when Tucker kissed her, all of her gave in. She wanted to let him take her to bed one more time, if that were to be their last time. They were both in sync in feeling that no more words were needed between them. Just touching and loving and holding on. But that's when the phone in the back pocket of Tucker's denim sounded. He quickly reacted to read the text, with intentions of throwing his phone onto the couch behind him and taking the woman he loved down the hallway to his bedroom. But the message was from Kate. She was on her way to drop off Livy.

"I'll go," was the last thing Remi said to him.

And in return, a deeply disappointed Tucker called out to her, "We are just beginning, Remi Jasper! Don't lose sight of that." He was not going to let her give up on them.

Chapter 18

She shouldn't have, but Remi watched Kate and Livy climb out of the their vehicle on Tucker's driveway. Kate sent Livy inside first, and then she trailed behind with two suitcases. Remi then watched Tucker come outside to carry a few clear plastic totes packed full of toys. To Remi, it looked as if Livy was moving back in permanently. She truly was overjoyed for Tucker, if that was the case. But, at the very same time, she wondered how long it would take for Kate to get her way and also move herself back into Tucker's home. Into his life again. And his bed.

Remi forced herself to step away from the window. She was hurt and angry. Life as she knew it had disappointed her once again. Any hope that she had for a long-term relationship with Tucker was crushed tonight. The three of them were a young family. There suddenly was no room for her. She couldn't stand in their way of getting back together and seizing an opportunity to share a future. She remembered how forlorn and heartbroken Tucker first appeared to be when she would watch their family outside of the very same window she now stood on the other side of again. *He had a chance to get his family back*. Sadly, Remi seemed to have forgotten how she once believed a woman like Kate did not deserve a man like Tucker.

∞∞

Kate stayed at the house for a long while to unpack both of Livy's suitcases and she placed all her clothing back inside the empty dresser drawers in Livy's bedroom. Tucker was working in there too, as he was helping Livy take all of her toys out of the plastic totes to place them somewhere in her room. Kate and Tucker talked very little to each other, but both paid attention to Livy's chatter – which was mostly questions and comments about taking all of her stuff out of Riley's house and bringing it back to her bedroom at her daddy's house. Kate had not explained to her yet that she would not see Riley again. Her move back to her daddy's house was a permanent one. If Kate had to find another place for her and Livy to live, she would. But she was not going to be in a hurry to look. She wanted to use her time to make a serious effort to win back Tucker's heart.

"I like all my stuff here," Livy commented, and Tucker tousled the blonde hair on top her head.

"Me too, kiddo." His little girl was back home indefinitely.

Kate smiled, too, as she left the room with the empty suitcases and placed them on the floor in the back of the hallway closet. That's where they were stored. She knew, because that used to be her home, too.

Tucker followed her out into the hallway and left Livy busy at play. She was content to be back home. Playing and just hanging out with her already didn't feel as rushed to Tucker. The feeling of having all the time in the world with his little girl again fulfilled his heart. He also knew that once Kate found another place of her own, Livy would again be uprooted. He had questions about her immediate plans. *Was she going back to stay at that mansion with Riley until he moved to San Diego?* "You didn't have to unpack, you know. I could have done it. I'm sure you've got a lot of your own stuff to move out of his house." Tucker didn't even want to speak Riley's name anymore. What a mess this had all become.

Kate shrugged. "Well I know where everything goes," she paused. "Livy seems really happy to be back here. I told her she didn't have to leave after two days this time. She can stay where she wants to be. She asked me if I was going to stay, too." Kate was playing the manipulative card.

"What did you tell her?" Tucker was not about to give in to her games. He hadn't been able to get his mind off Remi all night. It bothered him to know that she could see Kate's vehicle on his driveway, and she likely was thinking the worst.

"I didn't tell her that we are no longer going to share a home or our lives with Riley. That will just confuse her. I have to go back there to pack up my things, but I really don't want to do that when he's there. I'm going to stay at a hotel tonight, and I've taken a couple days off work this week to move out of his house."

"So, you're avoiding him?" Tucker completely ignored the mention of staying at a hotel, nor did he want to address where she planned to move her things. He was not about to invite her to stay there, not even for just one night. Not unless he wanted to see an abrupt end to his budding relationship with Remi.

"I told him I'm leaving him. We are done. There is nothing else to say."

"Not even if he buys a bigger diamond ring, or promises you a cruise around the world? I thought the gifts and the opportunities with him were endless..." Tucker was being spiteful, and Kate knew she deserved that.

"Not even," she simply replied. "I told you that I know what I want now."

"We're divorced, Kate."

She didn't address his comment, but she realized he must have followed up with the courthouse. "I need to tell Livy goodnight." She didn't move from where they stood in the hallway together. "Can I come by to see her tomorrow? I'll pick her up from school and bring her here after you're done for the day at Rix."

"Okay," Tucker stated.

Kate went back into Livy's bedroom to tell her goodbye. Livy didn't have more questions about where her mommy was going, or why she couldn't stay. She just assumed she would go back to Riley's house. And a small part of Kate actually contemplated going back there. It would have been a lot less lonely than a hotel room. But it was time to prove to Tucker that she was remorseful and worthy of another chance.

∞∞

After Livy was asleep, Tucker looked out of his living room window. Remi's house was all dark, but he knew she was still awake. She never went to bed early. He picked up his phone and called her.

Remi was lying in bed in a silent room. No television or music. Just her with her thoughts. She had seen Kate leave. She knew Tucker and Livy were alone in that house. That should have comforted her reeling mind, but it didn't. After the third ring, Remi gave in and answered Tucker's call.

"Hello Tucker."

"Hey… Liv's asleep. Can you come over? I would be on your doorstep right now, but I can't leave her." *He was a father first. Remi understood that.*

"I'm already in bed for the night."

"But you're not asleep. Run over here in your pj's, and sleep here tonight."

"I can't, Tucker." Remi gave no other excuse or explanation.

Tucker sighed on the opposite end of the phone. "Kate's not staying here. She's headed to a hotel, or who knows, maybe even back to that mansion where her things still are. She knows I chose you. I've made that very clear."

Remi momentarily closed her eyes. It would be so easy to fall back into him. "The three of you need time to see where this change in your lives is going to lead. I should stay back for awhile." Being a product of a broken family still affected her as an adult. If there ever was a chance for a child to grow up, happily with both parents together and under the same roof, Remi wanted that for anyone.

Tucker felt like throwing his phone across the room. Remi was hurt, and his messed-up life was the reason she had closed herself off again. "I know you want to do what seems like the right thing…" he paused to choose his words carefully, "but putting a family back together after deceit and distrust isn't always the answer." He could read her thoughts so well, and he wanted her to realize that not all families belonged together. Kate had ruined their chance for that. With her phone still pressed to her ear, Remi silently agreed, but again she willed herself to be strong and to keep her distance. Tucker relented. He wanted Remi there, with him. But he knew he shouldn't push her. "Are you okay over there alone? That kid hasn't tried to contact you, has he?"

"No. All is well." Surprisingly, Remi had not thought of Crue at all tonight. Her focus had been on the family across the street. And how things could change in the blink of an eye. She should know that all too well by now. Happiness was always short-lived.

"Remi, I'm here for any reason. Call me, day or night. I want you to be safe." He wanted to be the one to keep her safe.

"I know," was all she said in return. "Good night, Tucker. I'm happy that you have your little girl back."

He was too, but he didn't want his life to be in this frustrating limbo. It wasn't fair to Remi.

Chapter 19

Remi stepped into Principal Mike Kinsall's office before the first bell of the school day rang.

"Come in," he spoke with a smile. Remi walked up to his desk. "Good morning, Mr. Kinsall," Remi tried not to look or sound as nervous as she felt. She felt queasy this morning, and wished now that she had eaten breakfast. This man, wearing a white dress shirt and power red tie, was her boss. He was personable, but she had not really known him well, being a new employee and all. The rest of the staff had praised him though.

"Mike, remember? First names only here. No one is pulling rank on anyone." Mike chuckled, and Remi nodded her head with a smile. He offered her the chair in front of his desk and then the two of them sat down. "I apologize for taking so long to make this meeting happen. I was out all day yesterday."

"It's fine," Remi told him. "When I composed that email, this meeting felt more urgent than it does right now. I don't know how else to explain this to you, other than to just say it outright. I have a student who I counsel daily. Crue Macke, he's a senior. His father is dating Miss Pilgreen, um Rhonda," Remi corrected herself. "My first impression, and a few sessions thereafter, left me believing this young man had his act together. His homelife isn't easy, but I believed that Crue had a good handle on that." Mike Kinsall looked at her as if he wanted to say, *then what changed?* "Twice he has shown up at my house."

Remi watched her boss sit up straighter in his high-back leather chair, and he placed his elbows on his desktop. "What did he want?"

"To talk," she said. "I've repeatedly told him that I will not counsel him off the premises of this high school."

"And that hasn't sunk in?"

"My," she wanted to say boyfriend, but she couldn't bring herself to, "my neighbor was with me at the time of Crue's second visit. Crue seemed upset that I had a man inside of my house. He stated that he thought I was unattached. I've never spoken about that part of my personal life with him. I was thrown, and I'm sharing this with you to protect myself from something that could get out of hand. As the Director of Guidance, I've made the executive decision to appoint another counselor, aside from myself, for Crue."

The principal nodded. "I see. You think this young man is exhibiting some excessive behavior toward you, is that correct?"

"Yes, I do."

"I think you made the right decision, I do," Mike Kinsall stated, "and I will be calling Crue into my office today to talk to him about his behavior." Remi wondered if that was the best idea. Crue getting summoned to the principal's office, being reprimanded, and knowing that Remi reported him, could set him off. She heard Tucker's words ringing in her ears, *be safe.* "Have you talked to Rhonda about him?"

Here we go, Remi thought. The last thing she wanted to do was talk negatively about another member of the OTHS staff. "I have," Remi replied. "She thinks Crue is harmless, but I'm not sure how well she knows him. He has confided in me that he's uncomfortable around her, given her personal involvement with his father." The principal nodded. "Even if he is harmless, and I do hope that's the case," Remi explained, honestly, "showing up on my personal property after school hours is unacceptable. I want to protect my job, and my reputation."

"Absolutely," he agreed with Remi. And just as she was about to thank him for his time and attention, the bell rang and interrupted them. Their brief meeting had come to a close, but Remi believed it was productive.

Certain facts were hidden from her though. She was new to the community and the school district. She didn't have the privilege of knowing who was related as family, or connected as friends. Remi had no idea that Crue's father and Mike Kinsall had grown up together in this town. They were both starters on the basketball team that won the state championship twenty-five years ago. They were in each other's weddings. And Crue Macke was Mike Kinsall's godson. He did have an obligation to confront Crue, but it didn't exactly go the way Remi imagined it.

"You're eighteen, I remember what that was like. Just be careful. Find a girl closer to your own age, Crue. Stay away from Remi's house. You've alarmed her. Got it? Now, tell your dad he owes me a beer for covering your ass."

∞∞

Once the school day ended, Remi escaped to her home. She did not see Crue in the guidance office at all, and it was confirmed to her that he never showed up to be counseled. Remi wasn't surprised.

She poured herself a generous glass of white wine, and stood in front of her patio door. There was a sturdy screen on it, and she could feel the chilly autumn air coming inside the house. She held her glass, slid open the screen door, and stepped onto her deck in bare feet. She had yet to change out of her black pencil skirt and white flowy blouse. She tried not to think of Tucker, but she failed. His house was closed up when she drove into the neighborhood and glanced that way. No vehicles were on his driveway, but Remi knew that would change later. If Kate wanted him back, a woman like her would succeed eventually. She was too beautiful to be ignored or rejected too many times.

Remi thought about how she had checked her cell phone periodically throughout the day, but there were no messages from Tucker, which was *just as well,* she told herself. She couldn't help herself though. She wanted to share with him that she had a productive meeting with her principal today, and Crue had not been around her at all at school. But she had to get used to not having Tucker there to talk to her, to hold, and to love. Yes, she loved him. And, after only a month together, Remi already had lost him. It was her initial choice, she knew that, but Remi was adamant about giving Tucker the space to find his way back to his family. It's what was best for Livy.

Her second swallow of the wine made her stomach turn. She poured it out over the banister of the deck and into the grass. And when she walked back inside the house, she closed only the screen door. She didn't know what she needed more right now. To eat or to sleep. The latter, she decided, would allow her not to think about Tucker.

∞∞

Remi had no idea of the time passage. But when she woke up on the sofa, her living room was darkening, as the sun had almost entirely set. She immediately felt the chill in the air in the living room. She sat straight up and glanced toward the patio door. Just the screen separated her from near darkness. She swung her bare legs, still partially covered by a pencil skirt, off the sofa. And as she moved to plant her feet on the floor, Remi saw the armchair adjacent to her was occupied. Panic set in hard and fast.

"Crue! What the fuck are you doing?" Remi jumped to her feet so fast she instantly felt lightheaded. She willed off that feeling and ran around to the back of the sofa and stood behind it, as if it was some sort of barrier between her and him. *The unwanted high school kid in her living room.*

"Miss Jasper, your language surprises me," Crue spoke, as if he was the responsible adult. The clothes he wore were all dark. Black denim, black jacket, and calf-high biker boots. Gone were the flip-flops and torn denim that characterized him as a teenager. To Remi, the all-dark attire made him look dangerous.

His overgrown head of curls looked unkempt. Remi theorized that his entire appearance mirrored the confused and disarrayed state of his life. He clearly had unraveled right before Remi's eyes. From their initial meeting several weeks ago until now, he was a changed young man. A troubled soul. And, unfortunately, Remi felt as if she was past the point of helping him. But her life now depended on it. That, she knew for certain.

"You can't be here. I'm sure you are upset with me about talking to Mr. Kinsall, but it had to be done. Just do what he said and cease contact with me. Nothing more will have to be said or done. We can all just move on."

Crue smirked. "Mike is a good guy." Remi knew that Crue was referring to the principal, but the way he used his first name almost caught her breath. "He and my father go way back. He and my mother go even deeper." Remi creased her brow. "Yeah, it's a secret my mother told me only a few years ago when she was drunk and vulnerable. My dad, I mean the man who has raised me, doesn't know that my mother and his best friend were lovers. Mike Kinsall is my godfather and my daddy." Crue laughed out loud, and it sounded incredibly eerie.

"What?" Remi spat. "Does anyone else know besides you and your mother?"

Following a halfhearted shrug, he answered her. "If our respectable principal knows, he's not admitting anything to me." Crue winked. "It's fine, I don't need another daddy. In fact, I don't need the mother I have either. I am a man. I know what I want in my life." Remi's heartbeat quickened. Her cell phone was too far out of reach on the kitchen counter. If she had to make a run for it, she would use the open screen door, which was clearly how Crue had gotten in.

This craziness was all on Remi's hands now. Mr. Kinsall had been useless to her. There was no way to reach Tucker. She didn't even know if he was in close proximity, right across the street. Her only hope was to talk Crue down. *Just leave. Leave me alone.* Or to call the police. But again, her cell phone wasn't easily accessible. She would have to get herself outside and alert any one of her close-by neighbors to call 911.

"Aren't you going to counsel me, Miss Jasper? Ask me what I want? I'm a graduating senior. I should have a solid plan in place. College. Career. All that bullshit. Right? Go on, ask me..."

Remi inhaled a slow, deep breath through her nostrils. Her hands were placed on the back of the sofa, as an attempt to steady her shaky knees. "What do you want, Crue?" Her voice was intentionally strong. She didn't want him to know she was terrified. But her face must have revealed all that she felt and more when he answered her.

"You."

Chapter 20

As Tucker expected, Kate showed up early evening with Livy and she overstayed her welcome. He shook his head at how not so long ago she would sit idle in her vehicle outside on the driveway. Every drop-off and pick-up had to be quick. She had more important places to be. How suddenly things had changed. Life changed for Tucker too. He wanted Remi by his side. He missed her already. He needed an opportunity to see her, and soon. He was downright tempted to tell Kate she could hang out with Livy at the house tonight, but he was at a loss for a way to explain that to Livy – and even to Remi. He wanted to prove to her that Kate would keep her distance, as an ex-wife should. So, he was stuck there tonight. He did have a right to ask Kate what her plans were now. *Had she moved out of Riley's house yet, and where was she going to live?*

The three of them were in the kitchen. Livy was seated on a booster chair at the island. She was eating a slice of cheese pizza that Kate picked up as take-out for dinner on her way there. She thought ahead and ordered half the pizza as pepperoni and sausage. It was Tucker's favorite.

Kate stood near Livy, as it was typical of her not to sit down at mealtime. It kept her from the temptation to take a bite. Tucker wanted to roll his eyes. *For the love of God, just eat!* He opened the pizza box and took a slice. "You didn't have to, but thanks," was all he said. She smiled.

Once Livy finished eating, Kate helped her down so she could run off to play. She had been less needy toward Tucker. She already felt the reality and total ease of being home where she belonged. Nothing needed to be rushed anymore.

Tucker finished chewing before he spoke. "So what's your plan? Have you accomplished anything since yesterday?"

Kate halfheartedly shook her head. *How would she tell him that she had boxes of her belongings stashed in her vehicle now, with no place to unpack?* She managed to avoid Riley at the house, but she had given in and taken a phone call from him earlier today. He begged her to come back to him. He promised her they would find a way to somehow make living in both California and Illinois work. Everything Kate said went unheard by him. *I do not want to uproot Livy to that extreme. We aren't good for each other, not lifelong.* She basically implied *it was fun while it lasted. An exciting time until we attempted real life together.* Riley had not backed down. He demanded she stop and rethink her decision. And then he turned angry. He accused her of playing him for his wealth. Kate admitted she was drawn to the finer things, the lifestyle he lived. She admitted that it wasn't for her after all.

And then her final words to him were a lie. Or at least only wishful thoughts at this point. *"Tucker and I are back together. We are a family again with our daughter."*

"I moved out of Riley's house," Kate answered Tucker's question.

"And have you found a place?" Tucker realized he was being unreasonable if Kate had spent all day packing, there was no time to hunt for a place to live. That kind of thing didn't just happen overnight regardless. He assumed she had gotten a hotel room. And she had the night before. It was booked for her again tonight, just in case, but Kate intended to have other plans.

Before Kate could answer him, Tucker acted as if he heard something and he instantly reacted by getting off his stool at the island and moving quickly into the living room. The latch on the storm door clicked each time it was turned. At first, he thought his brother was there and had let himself in. A bigger hope he had was for it to be Remi.

Tucker rounded the corner to find Livy standing on her toes and pressed against the glass door. She had the door slightly open and was in the process of stepping outside.

"Liv!" he called out to her, and by now Kate was coming up behind him. "You know better than that. You can't go outside without me or mommy along. Besides, it's dark, honey."

"My blankie's in the car," Livy pouted.

"Oh her backpack is still out there," Kate noted. "We didn't carry it in, I guess. I had my hands full with the pizza and all." Kate backed into the kitchen to retrieve her keys as Tucker helped Livy step away from the door. She heard him say that he would go outside to get her backpack and the blanket.

When Kate entered the shared doorway of the kitchen and living room, she called out to Tucker, "keys!" He turned, and she threw them to him from across the room. He caught them in the air, and she saw him smile. It wasn't just a regular old smile. It was a genuine one. It was a memory-induced reaction. Kate and Tucker had this thing between them where everything was tossed. Tucker used to note, time and again, that she had a great arm. He would ask her, *What position did you play?* And then they both would laugh. Every single time. Because Kate never played a sport in her life. She was a princess. She didn't get sweaty unless she was at the gym, and in her adult life she preferred not to eat over getting exercise.

She waited for him to say it. To ask her, *what position she played…*

But he never did. Tucker certainly thought about their memory, but it didn't feel right to honor it anymore. He looked down at Livy and told her he would be right back.

It was something so small that once meant so much. The little things in life really were the meaningful things. And what a hard lesson learned that was for Kate. She stared at his back as he walked out the door.

ထထ

Tucker stepped out into the dark. The outside house lights lit up his path somewhat. He glanced across the street. It's what he did now. He wanted to be in her world. The window blinds were closed over there, and he could see light behind them. He walked the entire length of the driveway, as Kate's Suburban was parked directly behind his truck. When he made it to the back door, where Livy's car seat was, he reached for the handle just as he looked up at the street light between Remi's house and the neighbor next door. It was just a short distance down the road, but Tucker then noticed a parked car under it. It wasn't the neighbor's and it wasn't Remi's compact KIA. It was a blue coupe. And Tucker had seen that car only once before.

Chapter 21

Panic immediately rose to his chest. He almost dropped the keys in his hand and then quickly shoved them into the front pocket of his denim as he bolted across the street, taking long strides in his brown work boots on the rocks. He called out to Remi as he rang the doorbell three consecutive times. "Remi! Answer the door!" He hurriedly turned the handle, and discovered the door was locked.

On the other side of the door, Crue had been seated in the same armchair near the sofa where he watched Remi sleep when he first entered her house uninvited. Remi remained standing behind the sofa. At his insistence, she had just asked Crue what he wanted with his life. And his answer was her. Remi's eyes were wide and her face went pale. She was so lightheaded she could barely stand upright. She tried not to lock her knees, but the tension from her fear was physically battling against her.

Crue stood up abruptly. "Don't answer him!" He kept his voice low and his eyes looked both freaked and angry.

Remi was about to defy him, to save herself. This was going to be the only way, her only chance for help. Tucker could rescue her. He was a much bigger man than Crue, who was still just a lanky, broad-shouldered, overgrown kid. She opened her mouth to yell, and then she watched Crue pull a handgun from the backside of his pants.

He pointed it at her, and she knew as well as he did that he had no idea what he was doing. Remi assumed it wasn't even his gun, and his inexperience with it shushed her to complete silence. She would not yell. Not yet. She had to talk this boy down first. And fast, before Tucker gave up on her and left.

"Crue," she kept her voice low. "Put the gun down. I can let him in, and talk to him. You know," she held her breath, "I'll tell him I'm with you now." She could have thrown up in her mouth at that thought being a reality.

"You're just fucking with me. You don't mean it," Crue's words were tough, but Remi could see in his eyes that he was hopeful that she meant every single word. She had gotten to him. *Play along with this, Remi,* she told herself.

"No, I'm not. I'll lose my job, but we can make it work. I mean, if you really want to be together. We'll move away, somewhere far, where no one knows us. Come on, Crue. Let me open the door. I'll tell him the truth and then he'll leave." Tucker was still on the other side, frantically trying to get in. Kicking in the front window was his next thought.

"I'm doing this before you change your mind!" Crue shoved the gun back in his pants. And he pulled Remi over to the front door. She was so close to Tucker now that she could have cried. She had to hold herself together though. This was life or death. Hers and Tuckers. She knew it.

"Open the door, but I swear to you that I will shoot him if you try anything. I want him dead and out of your life anyway." Crue's eyes were both distant and fixed on Remi. She had never seen anyone like this. She knew Crue wasn't just contemplating doing something that crazy. He was crazy.

She turned the deadbolt and yanked open the door. Tucker had his shoulder against it and he was now just inches away from her. He wanted to reach for her. She wanted to fall into him. But Crue's presence had them both feeling frozen.

"Remi! Are you okay? What the hell is he doing here?" Tucker pulled on her arm now, noticing her pale face. He made a quick attempt to bring her closer to him and distance her from Crue. But she resisted. Crue watched her closely.

"He stopped by," Remi began to explain. She was adlibbing this performance and had only one chance to keep it believable for Crue, and to reach Tucker. She was counting on Tucker to read between the lines. He was an attentive listener, and Remi prayed that would benefit her now in this crisis. "You know he's my student that I told you about. I don't just counsel him. We're connected. We talk about our problems, and our hopes and dreams."

Tucker was listening raptly. He could see the fear in Remi's eyes, but her voice was strong. *That a girl. Play this crazy fucker. We will get him. Together.*

"I care about you, Tucker, I do," Remi inhaled a deep breath. Her head was spinning. "But you're with Kate again. There's no room for me in your life. And it's Crue that I want to be with now."

The mere thought of that being true sickened Tucker. But he, of course, knew better. He watched the body language of the young man behind Remi. He was a confident fool. An unstable one at that. "We can talk about this," Tucker spoke, momentarily not taking his eyes off Remi before he looked over at Crue. He clenched his jaw. "Why don't you give us some space? Go home for the night."

"No, he stays," Remi was quick to reply. "I think you should go, Tucker. I just want to call it a night, and get some sleep. You know how I always go to bed early." That was untrue, as Tucker knew well.

"You heard her!" Crue spoke up. "You need to be the one to go." Tucker did not budge. Feeling helpless on the other side of that locked door again was not going to happen to him.

"I'm not going anywhere," Tucker refused, and Remi tried to conceal her sigh of relief. Part of what she had said was true. He should be with his wife and child again. But now, most definitely was not the time that Remi wanted him to give up on her. Tucker saw the danger. Remi knew that. She was just scared out of her mind that his presence there was going to get him killed.

Crue didn't hesitate to retrieve his gun again. "Yes you are." He aimed it at Tucker. Tucker noticed how uncomfortable Crue was with holding the firearm. He clearly had not been a hunter, and he was too young to have a concealed carry license. Tucker also spotted the obvious, as Crue had not released the safety lock on the weapon. That was a good thing. But this kid's inexperience with the pistol frightened Tucker almost as much as if he would have known exactly what he was doing with it. Either way, Tucker had to protect Remi, and himself. And he had to get that gun from that kid before he hurt himself as well.

Tucker did not want this boy dead. He did want him in police custody. Locked up somewhere so he couldn't get to Remi ever again.

Tucker slowly lifted one hand in the air and held it up as a barrier between him and Crue. "Slow down, son."

"I'm not your son!" Crue spat at him, and his hand holding the gun was shaking almost uncontrollably.

"Right," Tucker appeased him. "It's just an expression. I didn't mean it literally. Just relax and realize what you're doing. If you care about Remi as you claim, put the gun down before she gets hurt."

"I would never hurt her!" Crue yelled. The wild mop of curls on his head was matted from perspiration. Tucker prayed to God that his voice had carried and someone in the neighborhood would be alerted to this insanity. *Namely, Kate. She must have looked for him outside on the driveway by now.*

"I know that," Remi's soothing voice broke their intense argument. Crue glanced at her, and Tucker only watched the unsteady weapon in his hand. *Keep talking to him. Keep his mind on you.* Tucker willed his thoughts to Remi. He trusted how perceptive she could be. She was well aware of what was going on here. Crue could be overtaken if he was distracted. "Of course you would never hurt me. You love me, right Crue?"

Crue's hand was trembling, and he steadied it with his opposite hand. The gun was still aimed at Tucker, just a few feet away. And Tucker's eyes had gone to the safety lock again. Still untouched. He assumed and hoped with his life that Crue was clueless. He couldn't effectively pull the trigger just yet. But it would only take a second to unlatch it. And Tucker would need that costly second if Crue were to react and ready himself to pull the trigger on him.

Crue took his eyes off Tucker and watched Remi. She wasn't done talking to him yet. "You want to be together, right?" Remi's words were convincing. Crue completely believed her deceit.

He nodded repeatedly before he spoke. "Yeah, um yes, I want you in my life. You're the only one who gets me. I can talk to you about anything. There's no one else like that for me. My feelings are real. I can't stay away from you. You told me to stay away. I thought you meant that…" Crue was rambling. Tucker had his eyes on the gun. It was time to make the move to grab it. Now. And fast.

Tucker had been entirely focused on the gun and the prospect of lunging toward a distracted Crue to get the weapon away from him that it had gone unnoticed to him how Remi was losing her focus. Her eyes blurred. Sweat beads had formed on her forehead and around her lips. She swallowed hard. She brushed back the damp hair from her neck.

In the moment Tucker charged and swiped the gun out of Crue's grip, Remi went down. She hit the floor and instantly lost consciousness.

Chapter 22

Tucker was still in disbelief. He sat alone in the waiting room of Memorial East in Shiloh, Illinois. The ambulance had taken a now-conscious Remi to the hospital. He wanted to ride with her, but he was dealing with the police, who finally had Crue Macke in their custody. And his attention had also been focused on Kate and his little girl. Kate needed to get back to the house, to Livy. She had left her for what was supposed to only be for a brief moment to check on Tucker outside. Kate hung her head out of the storm door and could not see him. And that's when she heard and then saw the intense, dangerous commotion across the street. Tucker had left the main front door to Remi's house wide open. She could see directly inside through the glass storm door. And Kate was the one who called 911.

Tucker leaned forward and rested his elbows on his quads. He closed his eyes and rubbed his face with his open palms. And when he sat upright again, his brother stood directly in front of him.

"Chase. You got my message."

"Hell yes. What is going on with you? A crazy kid is obsessed with your neighbor, and held a gun to you?" Chase found the chair beside his little brother. He assumed he needed to sit down for this story.

"That's it, really. Remi counseled him at school. He lost his mind over her. He's sort of been stalking her. And tonight he got into her house through the back door, where she had the screen open. I spotted his car parked down the street, and raced over there."

"Ahh, you're the lady's knight in shining armor," Chase teased him.

"I was terrified, bro. I really thought that crazed idiot had done something to hurt her."

Chase leaned closer to Tucker. "You really care about her. Not just for her safety."

"I told you that I did. I love her, and she loves me. But dammit, she's pushing me away because Kate's back."

"What? Back? She left you." Chase thought they were divorced, or close to it. This was exactly like his former sister-in-law to toy with his brother's emotions again.

"She left her new man. He wanted her to drop everything and move to San Diego where there's apparently a job opportunity of a lifetime for him. He's a selfish asshole and he wanted Kate and Livy to change their lives just to be with him."

Chase shook his head. "If you tell me that you are considering taking her back, I am going to walk out of here right now. I will not support you on that. Never. Brother or not, I'll be done with you."

"Why?" Tucker pressed him. He wanted to process what he knew he needed to hear. For his entire life he had trusted his brother more than anyone.

"You have never been good enough for her. And I'm sorry if this is hurtful, but you never will be. Kate needs what we all thought she had found – a wealthy man who lavished her with everything money can buy. I doubt she even loved him." Tucker thought about that. And he was quick to conclude that Kate believed she loved him. She at least wanted to convince herself of it. Regardless, it was Riley Ratchford's lifestyle that she was swayed by and fell for. "You're suddenly good enough now. Can't you see that?" Chase asked his brother. "You're better than that. You deserve more. You will find a woman who loves you for you."

"I already have," Tucker stated, and Chase nodded in acceptance. "Now I just need a doctor to come in here and tell me she's going to be okay."

ꝏꝏ

Remi listened to Dr. Tom Horton, an older man with large, round glasses perched low on the bridge of his nose. "Your bloodwork was conclusive," he stated, and Remi felt foolish for not eating all day, which likely had caused the low blood sugar that she was prone to have, and then she consequently passed out. In addition to that, she had been emotionally near hysterics by Crue's presence in her home. His words and his actions had terrified her. *He wanted her. He had a gun. He wished Tucker dead.* It was all just too much. *No wonder she had lost consciousness. It was probably an involuntary coping mechanism.*

"Miss Jasper, you're pregnant."

Remi put a hand to her mouth. She thought she was going to be physically sick. *Pregnant?* "No, that can't be. I always have light periods, and I just had one last week, or the week before." *Well, sort of,* she thought. *It had been extremely light, even compared to what was a typical cycle for her.*

"You will need to get checked out by an obstetrician as soon as possible," Dr. Horton advised her, as he patted her hand now on her lap. "The shock will wear off and you'll be a happy mommy-to-be. I'm sure of it." He smiled. Remi wasn't so sure of it, or anything else for that matter. *Tucker was going back to his family. He already had a child. He would be upset with her for assuring him that she was on birth control, and yet it had been ineffective.*

"Right. Um. Thanks doctor. And here I was expecting to get scolded for trying to function on an empty stomach." She tried to laugh, but the humor in this shocking situation for her never came.

"Best take better care of yourself," the doctor spoke, "as you now have a little one to nurture."

Remi only nodded, because speaking this seemed too unreal. And as the doctor walked out, she heard him say he would track down the baby's father in the waiting room. *Tucker!*

Remi rung her hands out on her lap as she otherwise sat strangely still on that hospital bed. This was lifechanging. *Could she really raise a baby alone?* Practically her entire life she had been used to living it all by herself. And now, there would be someone else who counted on her. *This baby. Her baby. Tucker's baby.* Remi had a decision to make. *Would she tell him? Or was it time to move on with her life again, to take it in another different direction?* There was always the option for her to return to Monticello, Indiana. All she knew for sure was she could not stay and raise Tucker's baby in the same neighborhood and directly across the street from where he lived with his first family.

Chase stayed with Tucker long enough to get the good news from the doctor. *Remi was going to be alright. The state of her health was not threatened in any serious way.* Tucker, who was beside himself with relief, asked if he could see her.

He turned the door handle and entered her room. He stood there for a moment, just staring at her. She watched his face break into a smile and his eyes looked watery. "I've never in my life been so happy to see someone as I am right now. You're okay. Thank God, you're okay, Rem." Remi let out of slight giggle as he made his way over to her and sat down beside her on the bed. He wrapped his arms around her, and she fell into his chest. For the first time in a very long time, and ever in front of Tucker, she cried. Her sobs and constant tears were for this man she loved and still could lose. And for their baby who deserved both parents in its life. Especially to be loved by a father like Tucker. She couldn't rob him of that chance. But she needed some time before she told him the truth.

Tucker held her, believing her breakdown in his arms had everything to do with the trauma that Crue had put her through. "I don't know what I would have done if he had hurt you," Tucker spoke in her ear, and Remi knew what he had assumed. "It's okay now. You're safe. He's gone. Just cry it out. I'm here. I'm always going to be here for you."

Remi backed herself out of his arms, and he stayed close beside her. "I was so scared for myself and for you. He wanted to kill you. He told me he would."

"Stop, it's over. He had no idea what he was doing with that gun. I had the better chance, the upper-hand the whole time."

Remi rolled her eyes through her tears. "Don't be such a tough guy. You were scared, too."

"Absolutely," Tucker agreed.

"So, the police, they locked him up? He's actually in jail?" Remi asked. The last thing she had witnessed was Crue pinned to the floor by Tucker, and an officer of the law had pulled him to his feet and cuffed his hands behind his back. *You have to help me…* were Crue's last words to Remi, as she was on a gurney once she had regained consciousness and had the undivided assistance of the paramedics still near her. She only looked away from him. She didn't have to respond. Nor did she want to.

"He's in custody, yes," Tucker reassured her. "Try not to focus on anything more than that concerning him. We know he's a troubled kid, but after tonight he's also a criminal."

Remi stayed silent.

"Did the doctor say why you passed out like that?" he asked. "All he told me was that you're okay, you're healthy."

"Empty stomach, low blood sugar. Nothing alarming," Remi lied.

"Good," Tucker touched her hand. "I'll take you home after they give you the okay to leave." Remi had been admitted as a patient upon arrival as she had been given fluids via an IV and a blood test was ordered.

"I could call an Uber if you don't want to wait," she told him.

"I want to wait," he still held her hand in his. "And while we are waiting on this bed together, I have something to say. And you're going to listen. No interruptions. Just good listening and comprehension. Got it?" Remi smiled at him, and he chuckled at himself. "My ex-wife's life is suddenly in limbo. My child is living with me full-time again because her mother and I both agree that she needs some solid stability in her little life. The only thing that has changed for me is Livy now needs me to be there for her more than I was able to be when she moved out with her mother. That's all. I look out my windows and wonder what you're doing over there in that house all alone. I constantly check my phone for messages from you. I miss looking into the most beautiful dark brown eyes I have ever seen. I want to talk to you and hold you before we close our eyes to sleep every single night for the rest of our lives."

Remi wanted to let her tears freefall again, but she willed herself not to this time. "Tucker, you are getting way ahead of yourself. We were just getting started, but then things changed."

"I'm not going to let you do that," Tucker interrupted her. "You think I'm getting ahead of myself? I'm not. We're not. We both willingly and effortlessly fell in line with something so natural. We went with how we felt and what we wanted. And I know I still want you in my life. Please, Remi. Just give in. Just like you did before. I'm trying like all hell to chisel away at the wall you've put back up and all around yourself again. Just be with me and love me as much as I love you."

There were tears rolling off her face now. No one had ever said anything like that to her before. Remi Jasper wasn't loved that way. She never felt needed or wanted to that intense and fulfilling degree.

"I love you, too," she told him back for the very first time.

"You do?" Tucker partly teased her. And he already wanted to hear her tell him those words again.

Remi nodded her head. "I heard your every word, I did," she began. "I want you in my life more than you will ever know. I just need some time to sort through a few things in my heart. Can you give me that?"

Tucker wasn't entirely sure what she was asking of him. Or what she could possibly have to sift through in her mind and heart. He still feared she was offering him a way out, the chance to reunite with Kate and as a family with Livy. He gave in. This had to be enough for him for awhile. He would wait for Remi to be ready, if that's what she wanted him to do.

He leaned into her and he kissed her hard and full on the lips. She responded. Physically resisting him had proven to be her greatest weakness. And finally, leaving her breathless, he pulled away from her, and moved off the bed.

"I'll wait," he told her. "Now I'm going to get you home." Tucker left the room to seek Remi's discharge papers at the nurse's station.

Remi sat back on the bed and placed her hand over her abdomen. Tucker needed to know about their baby. She just couldn't bring herself to tell him. Not yet. She wouldn't use a baby as a crutch. Or as a means to snare him. They had to be able to stand on their own together. They were friends and lovers, brand new to each other. Remi wanted to believe she and Tucker were strong and rock solid enough to last forever. She never wanted a child of her own to have his or her family broken. Remi personally suffered that loss and its repercussions. Now, Crue was going through it as a teenager and unable to mentally deal with it in a healthy way. And even little Livy was forced to understand the confusion of something gone wrong between two people who vowed to love each other forever.

Chapter 23

Tucker practically waltzed up to the nurse's station. All he wanted to do was get Remi out of there, and take her home. He already texted Kate from the waiting room earlier and told her that he was staying with Remi tonight, whether she remained in the hospital or went home. At first, Kate's only response was, *okay.* And then she asked what Tucker really didn't have a choice but to agree. *Am I staying at the house with Livy?* She didn't want to take her back to the hotel, nor did she want to deal with unloading her things from the back of her vehicle. It was too late at night, and Livy was already asleep. Tucker realized all of that, and allowed Kate to stay. He knew this would bother Remi, but he hoped having him stay with her all night long would redeem him.

One of the nurses looked up from her computer, and smiled. "Tucker Brandt, it's been a long time." Tucker recognized the nurse as a high school classmate. Missy Lammers. She had crushed on both him and his brother. Chase never said exactly how far he had gotten with her in the bed of his pickup truck. Tucker chuckled to himself. She was still a pretty one.

"It sure has, Missy. How are you?"

"Good. Real good," she said, standing to meet him on the opposite side of the counter. The nurse working with her there just smiled, took a clipboard chart off the wall, and walked away. "I hear you're divorced, and possibly attached again?"

Damn, word traveled around that city ridiculously fast, Tucker thought, but truly did not care. "I'm with the beautiful woman in Room 22 and I'd like to get her out of here."

Missy smiled. "I'll get you the paperwork. We don't want to keep your baby mama waiting."

Tucker focused hard on the nurse in front of him. The wild girl from high school. *What had she just said to him?* "No. Remi Jasper is in Room 22. You're confusing her with someone else."

Missy eyes widened. "Oh gosh. You don't know. I'm going to get myself fired if I keep talking right now."

"Keep talking," Tucker all but ordered her. "Are you for certain about this? Remi is pregnant?"

"I read her chart," the nurse kept her voice low. "Dr. Horton confirmed the pregnancy with a blood test. It's why she fainted."

At this moment, Tucker could have fainted. Or dropped dead. *Remi kept the truth from him. She lied to him.* He tried to tell himself that she must be scared of out her mind. But he wasn't going to make excuses for her. He had a right to know that she was carrying his baby. Tucker was hurt and angry.

ꝏꝏ

I need to make a quick stop at the grocery store," Tucker said, as they drove on US Route 50, close to Schnucks, where Tucker often shopped for just himself and Livy.

"Okay," Remi said, wondering if Livy needed something back at his house. It was late, and she should have been in bed. "I really don't want to wait in the truck alone in a dark parking lot. Do you mind if I tag along with you inside?" Remi was still shaken by Crue's actions tonight. She knew she was safe now, but the thought of being alone frightened her more than she wanted to admit. She was relieved that Tucker was planning to stay with her.

"Not at all," Tucker replied, and the two of them were silent again until they entered the grocery store.

"I just need two things," Tucker said as he passed up the grocery carts and walked side by side with Remi. He never said what those two things were.

They skipped over what felt like every aisle until Tucker finally turned down one. Remi never asked what he was looking for. He stopped when he spotted the pickle jars. "Spears or whole?" he asked her.

"Um, whole I guess. Why am I choosing?" Tucker only shrugged his shoulders as he took the jar of whole pickles off the shelf and walked on.

He looked back at her. "You coming?"

"Yeah," she told him as she picked up her pace to meet him at the end of the aisle. After that, they walked clear across the store to the frozen section. Tucker stopped at the ice cream. "Chocolate or vanilla? Or something more sinful?"

"Vanilla, but why are you—" Remi looked down at his hands. Pickles and ice cream. Her eyes widened. *How did he know? And why wasn't he angry with her? And did they really have to wait until they made it through the check-out lane and all the way back outside to the truck in the parking lot to talk about this?*

Yes, they did.

Once they both were seated in the truck, Tucker waited to turn over the engine. Only the dome light was dimmed above them, but they could still see each other's faces.

He turned to her. She looked back at him. She really did not know what to say. She felt awful for lying to him. And then Tucker broke the building tension and spoke first. "When were you going to tell me? I don't want to believe that you were going to keep this from me, or that you would ever consider doing something drastic."

Remi shook her head. She would never. "I needed time to think. I wanted you to know. I just didn't know how to tell you, or what to expect of you. This was very much a shock to me, too. My trusty contraception clearly failed me. I don't have an explanation, I'm sorry, Tucker."

"This is my doing as much as yours," Tucker spoke genuinely. "I want this baby, our baby. We made he or she out of love, and I know that sounds like an old corny cliché because sex will knock up a woman just the same as making love, but dammit Remi I love you and we deserve the chance to have a happy life together. Our baby deserves that, too."

She laughed out loud. It was more of nervous giggle, but she laughed nonetheless. "What's so funny?" Tucker wanted to know.

"That you knocked me up. I'm thirty years old and I'm going to have a baby. I didn't know if that would ever happen for me. I do want to be happy, Tucker. I already know you'll be the most loving daddy."

He smiled. "I'm happy now. With you. And this right here," he tapped his fingers on the plastic bag of pickles and ice cream on the counsel between them, "is my way of showing you that whatever you need from me, you will get. I want to be there for you every single day along the way."

Remi tried to hold back her tears. Tucker caught one of them with his thumb on her cheek. "I never realized you were such a crier," he teased.

"Hormones," she reminded him with an eye roll.

"Ahh…this is going to be fun."

He chuckled and she swatted her hand to his chest. And then he pulled her into him, with the pickles and ice cream between them, and he kissed her.

Chapter 24

Kate waited to hear from Tucker, but she hadn't in hours. The only text message she received was one that she didn't reply to. It was from Riley.

Last call. My jet, which could be our jet, leaves first thing in the morning. Reconsider.

She read his words twice. Despite everything, Riley still wanted her. And given what took place across the street tonight, and how Tucker had chosen to be by Remi's side, Kate was teetering on that fine line. *All of her things were literally stuffed into the back of her vehicle. She was homeless. Livy was well taken care of. She was back in familiar surroundings with Tucker. But where had that left Kate? Could she really pick herself up and carry on, alone? Or should she seize that life of luxury that awaited her? She could jet to Livy anytime.*

She was lying on her side of the bed. That queen-size space she once shared with her husband. Those rose-colored sheets were still the same. So much about that house was unchanged. That's the way Tucker was designed. There was no need to replace anything that wasn't tattered or broken beyond repair. He had replaced her though. She never thought he would that quickly, but he had. And that reality sunk in hard and fast for Kate tonight. Her entire future hung in the balance. She willingly and carelessly gave up her old life, and there was no getting it back. She needed to talk to Tucker one more time before sunrise. She sent him a text before she turned off the light in their old bedroom.

Can we talk? It's important.

Just as she moved between the sheets onto her side, she placed her open palm on Tucker's pillow, and then she heard the front door to the house open. That latch on the storm door always clicked.

Kate threw off the sheet and duvet that covered her, and planted her bare feet on the floor. She was wearing pale pink pajama bottoms and a matching tank top. She stopped mid room when she heard voices. *Tucker was not alone. He brought her along. Of course he did.*

She forced herself to hold her head up high and walk out of their old bedroom. Tucker had turned on a lamp in the living room, and Remi sat down on the end of the sectional. They both saw Kate walking down the hallway, and from which room she had been in. Tucker held his breath at that thought, knowing that Remi was also well aware of how bold Kate could be.

Kate folded her arms across her chest. She wasn't wearing a bra. It was the middle of the night. Regardless, Kate was fully confident with her body in front of anyone. *Maybe especially in the company of the new woman in Tucker's life.*

"Sorry to wake you," Tucker said, and this whole scenario felt unbelievable. Kate was back in his house – and how obvious had it been that she was sleeping in their old bed. Remi was having his baby. Livy was again in his life full-time. He needed to stop his mind from reeling. He craved sleep, but as he had told Remi, he wanted to set some ground rules among the three of them. He was going to put an end to Remi's insecurities as well as Kate's false hope.

"You didn't wake me," Kate said. "I have not been able to sleep. I actually just texted you." She acknowledged Remi now. "Are you okay?" Kate knew she had not been hurt, but the paramedics were concerned enough to take her to the hospital once she had lost and then regained consciousness. Tucker felt a little proud of Kate right now. She was showing kindness and concern for Remi. At least he hoped she was genuine.

Remi nodded. "I'm fine now, thank you." She offered no more information. That ball was appropriately in Tucker's court.

"That's actually why we are back here so late," Tucker spoke in turn. "We need to discuss some things." Tucker remained standing near the end of the sofa where Remi was seated. And Kate stood in the middle of the living room. She nodded. Her long blonde hair was down and reached past her shoulders and halfway down her back. Remi thought she looked like a model for Victoria's Secret sleepwear. *Disheveled but sexy.* Remi pondered if Tucker had been out of his mind to choose her over a goddess of beauty like Kate. Remi forced her insecurities aside because he wanted her. And it was time she appreciated that.

"We're divorced, Kate. While I do want us to get along and have open communication, for Livy's sake, I also want to set some boundaries. I'm with Remi now. My time will be shared between her and my daughter. I realize you are in a fog of change right now, but soon you will be settled in a place of your own and ready to move on with your life." Kate remained expressionless. If Tucker thought any lone house or apartment of her own nearby was going to appease her, he didn't really know her after all. If she couldn't have him and the life that she foolishly took for granted, she wanted more of everything else. And this time love had nothing to do with it.

"Of course," Kate choked out the words. "I agree. And I will respect that you are moving on." This time, her words were hardly genuine.

"Thank you. There's more," Tucker looked down at Remi and reached for her hand. There was no other way to tell Kate their news, other than to just say it. "Remi fainted tonight because she's pregnant. She and I are going to have a baby…"

Kate's arms dropped from her chest. She had been contemplating making a major, life-changing decision tonight. She was uncertain and indecisive. Sometimes in a circumstance like this, she needed a sign. Something, anything, to push her to take that leap. She had one now.

Recovering from feeling as if someone knocked the wind out of her, Kate forced herself to respond. "I don't know what to say," she admitted. "Congratulations seems so empty coming from the ex-wife, doesn't it? You're going to have another child?" *Someone needed to wake her from this nightmarish hell she was living in lately.* "Well I hope Remi knows there's no better daddy out there for her baby. I would know." Kate made fleeting eye contact with Remi, and Remi attempted a warm smile. *What else could she do?*

Tucker ignored her compliment. It was time for him and Remi to leave. This truth would set Kate free, he believed. She needed to know that her intimate part in his life was over. He had certainly proved that to Remi tonight, and he wholeheartedly believed she was finally ready to commit to him.

"We should go then," Tucker said, and Remi stood. She was ready to leave. To say it had been a long night for her was an understatement.

"Wait," Kate spoke, primarily to Tucker but at this point she no longer cared if Remi listened in. "About that text I sent. I have something to tell you, and now it can't wait until morning."

"Go ahead," Tucker told her, and he had absolutely no idea what was about to hit him. Once again, Kate was going to disappoint him. This time, beyond measure.

"I know where I'm headed with that packed vehicle on your driveway," she began. Tucker waited to hear that she was going to buy a larger and fancier home than what they owned and shared together. It was always the same song and dance with her. "To the airport. I'm going to San Diego with Riley."

Tucker tried not to raise his voice, because Livy was asleep just down the hallway. But anger had risen in his chest. It was just like Kate to spite him. To make a reckless decision that she would regret later. This would hurt him, she knew that, but above all else, it was going to greatly affect Livy the most. "What in the hell are you telling me? You are not taking Livy to live halfway across the country! You said so yourself that the whole idea was insane and never going to happen! Are you that upset about my relationship with Remi? Are you angry that she and I are going to have a baby? There are more sensible ways to deal with life not going in your favor!" Tucker had gone on endlessly, expressing his shock and anger and disapproval of Kate's ridiculous decision. She only stood there. And she let him speak.

"I will let the two of you talk," Remi interjected, but Tucker stopped her. His head was spinning, but he had to focus on Remi for a moment. "Wait. I don't want you to go into your house alone."

Remi didn't want that either. "I'll be in the kitchen," she said, hoping the two of them could keep their voices down. She certainly wouldn't try to overhear them. This was between Tucker and Kate now. All Remi could do was hope Kate was not going to take Livy that far away from her father. Because that would destroy him.

"Just listen to me," Kate spoke, as she stepped closer to Tucker. She could lessen the distance between them now, as his new love was no longer in the room. "I said I was going, not Livy."

Tucker's face fell. "You're leaving her? Abandoning our little girl?"

Kate felt tears flood over her eyes. "No," she stated. "I will be jetting back and forth like a madwoman to see her and spend time with her. I won't uproot her or put her through the travel. Not yet. Not until she's a little older."

"But you're leaving her? You are leaving her here with me. How can you do that? How is it even remotely okay in your mind —and in your heart— to walk away from your child like that? You said you will see her and spend time with her? She's your child, not an old friend for chrissakes!" Tucker's voice carried out of that room.

Kate allowed the tears to freefall from her eyes, and she never brushed them off her face. She wanted to ask him to give her a reason to stay. To be that reason. But she couldn't. Not anymore, as she lost that privilege and he had moved on. "I don't have much left here anymore," she admitted what she truly believed. "I had the world when I was in your arms, and I couldn't see it. It wasn't enough. I had to foolishly chase after what I thought I was missing, what I believed I needed. If I cannot have real, genuine love, then I want everything else that money can buy."

Tucker shook his head at her. He was purely disgusted. She was now a disgraceful excuse for a human being in his eyes. "I thought I knew you, and then you crushed my heart. The funny thing is..." he paused, because he felt like he was breaking inside. His pain was for Livy. "I defended you. No matter how badly I hurt, or how absurd I believed your decision was to leave me and our family, I said more than once that you were a good mother. And now this? You're doing this to Livy? I don't know how you will live with yourself."

Kate didn't either. "I will be back for her weekly. She's not even going to have time to miss me in between visits." She had it all planned. "I have to do this, Tucker. I can't stay here and watch you play house with another woman, and a new baby. Livy is going to be a big sister," she choked on a sob. She had the nerve to blame him for her shocking decision. Tucker only stared at her. There wasn't anything left for him to say.

Chapter 25

"I don't know what to say," Remi admitted, in an attempt to reach Tucker and encourage him to open up to her. Silence was unlike him. He had been all to himself, lost in thought —and anger and disappointment— since they left his house in the middle of the night and walked back across the street. They laid in her bed now, in the dark, close but not touching. "I'm still holding a grudge toward my father for not being there for me since I was eleven years old," Remi began. "I'm probably too close to this issue to have an unbiased opinion." A part of her had wanted to get in Kate's face and forewarn her of the amount of pain and heartbreak she would cause her child. Distance was never good for anyone's soul, especially a child.

Tucker remained still on his back, staring up at the ceiling. He was in such turmoil over Kate's sudden and drastic decision. "There you go," he finally spoke. "You assumed abandonment. You see Kate's choice as she's leaving Livy. Why can't she see it that way? Sure, she will be jetting back and forth multiple times a week like a crazy person, she will still see Livy and be with Livy – but where? She'll hang out at a hotel with her? Her wealthy lover will buy her another home for the sole purpose of living in it only when she's in town? What happens when Livy cries out for her mommy in the middle of the night? When she's sick? Or scared? A three-hour flight from there to here is too damn far away!"

"You'll be there for her," Remi spoke to him. "You're not her mommy, but you are her daddy. And from what I've seen, that does not mean you're second best to Livy. The two of you have the most special bond. She will turn to you as I have seen her do, because she knows you will be there. Because she adores you. Because she feels your love, and the security that you provide. You are very nurturing with her." Remi paused for a moment, unsure if she should go on. "And then there's me. I'm new to Livy's life, but I want to be there for her, for a lifetime, if she'll have me."

Tucker turned to Remi. "Listen to you…" he smiled. "Careful there. You are beginning to sound as if you are ready to grab ahold of this life that's been blatantly paved in front of us in such a short amount of time. No second guessing anymore?" he asked her. "No insecurities or ridiculous feelings of not being worthy of happiness? It's not going to be all rainbows and unicorns," he chuckled mid words, "but I promise you, the groundwork for us is love and happiness. We may have to dig back down to the foundation sometimes to find it and to remind ourselves of our stability, but it's always going to be just under our feet."

"Holding us up," Remi added, feeling surprisingly confident. And Tucker looked as if he had found his footing again. No matter what lie ahead, they were going to be together. They would be a family with Livy – and their new baby on the way.

ꝏꝏ

Kate was alone on the immense private jet that sat idle on the runway. She watched out the window as a staff of at least a half a dozen unloaded her things from the back of her Suburban. Clothes, shoes, and some personal items. Riley had arranged for the help. All of it would be packed and on board with them. The only thing Kate was instructed to do was wait for him. Riley Ratchford was taking care of her. She didn't have to plan or prepare. She was drinking a mimosa at six-thirty in the morning. The man who showed her to the plane had asked if she wanted anything, anything at all, for breakfast or from the well-stocked wet bar. Kate wasn't shy about requesting a drink. *Double the alcohol,* she contemplated saying, but she refrained.

This was the life! Kate told herself as her cocktail gradually numbed the rest of her feelings. Every two days. That's how often she would see Livy. Riley had kept and gifted his huge house to them, still fully furnished and ready for Kate and Livy's frequent stays there. Kate wasn't sure how she felt about that house being permanently theirs but it was something that was done for her. Riley made her life easy, and all of his efforts were extravagant. There was no limit now to anything that she wanted. What she needed, however, was lost to her. Kate took a long swallow from the tall glass.

She turned back, away from the window, and saw Riley standing near the entrance to their private quarters. He had just boarded the jet. Black dress pants, black button-down long-sleeve shirt, black loafers. His blond hair was perfectly styled with those same side-swept bangs.

"You have no idea how pleased you've made me," Riley said to her, and he reached out his arms. Kate set her drink aside and stood up. Her head was foggy from the early morning alcohol on an empty stomach. She went to him, and he pulled her into his arms. "It doesn't matter why you changed your mind, alright? All that matters now is you're here, you are with me, and this life we are going to have together will be absolutely incredible. Anything that you want is yours!"

Love. Attention. Trust. And all the little things she took for granted, that once brought priceless joy to her life, were gone.

Not anything, Kate clinched.

Fortune and prestige, however, had called her name lifelong. And it was time that she seized the opportunity to make it her first priority. Heartbreak, at no fault but her own, had led her to this place.

Chapter 26

A walk through Hidden Lake Winery in rural Aviston, Illinois, just twenty miles east of O'Fallon, was Tucker's idea. It was the early days of autumn and the leaves had turned stunning colors, leaving the backdrop of that silent wooded forest looking picture perfect. While Remi was twelve weeks pregnant and could not indulge in the wine-making culture of the area, she was happy to be there with Tucker. He held her hand as they walked. She noticed earlier the same pressed jeans and white long-sleeve button down oxford shirt and gray pointed-toe boots that he wore on their first date. That was the night she had gotten to know him and instantly fell for him. He could say the same for her.

The air was cool out there, and Remi pulled together her extra-long off-white cardigan sweater which she wore with elastic-waisted skinny black pants and black block-heeled booties. Tucker hadn't mentioned their plans to Remi, as he had only told her they were going to take a stroll on the grounds of the winery before dinner.

Remi hooked her arm through his and he turned to kiss her forehead. "It's beautiful out here," she said, feeling relaxed with him. And happy. She was truly content to be his. She didn't have any doubts anymore.

"I know, that's why I wanted to bring you here. This time of the year it's really something to see."

"Wish I could have a glass of wine," she teased.

"We'll come back again," he said, implying after the baby was born. Remi smiled at the thought of them having a baby and being a family — with Livy too.

Up ahead, Remi noticed a white-haired man in a black overcoat. She never said anything, in fear of being overheard, and Tucker had just kept walking with her, toward him. When they were about ten feet away, Tucker and the man in black shared nods. And then Tucker turned to Remi.

"This is Jack. He's a minister. He has performed hundreds of wedding ceremonies out here in the woods. Remi made a polite effort to smile at Jack. She had been oblivious to Tucker's plan, but then her eyes widened at the realization.

Tucker chuckled, partly because he was happy to have gotten her this far, and to pull off the special surprise he had planned. And also because he was a little nervous. He turned toward her, and reached for both of her hands. Hers were cold and his warm, masculine hands instantly comforted her. And then he bent down to one knee. Remi released her hands from his and covered her mouth with an open palm. Tucker held up a little black velvet box with the most beautiful pear-shaped diamond, spotted by two tiny emeralds. "I'm not sure if any man has ever proposed marriage and actually had the minister on hand to seal the deal," he began with a wide smile on his face, "but we've never done things the typical way, so why start now?" Remi laughed through her tears. She would say yes to forever with him and commit to him right here and now. "Remi Jasper, I've loved you from the very beginning of our relationship. We were neighbors for a few weeks, and friends only for a matter of hours before we knew we belonged together as lovers and soul mates." Tucker had tears in his eyes, Remi's were already streaming down her face. "Do me the lifetime honor of being my wife. Marry me, Remi…"

She nodded through her tears and accepted his marriage proposal in between sobs. Tucker was on his feet now, and he pulled her into his arms and kissed her. The minister waited until they turned to him. And when they did, he began the most intimate wedding ceremony. It didn't matter to Remi that she wasn't wearing a traditional wedding dress with flowers in hand. She had ironically chosen to wear a flowy off-white sweater. They also paid no mind to having no attendants or guests. All they needed was each other.

When it was time to recite their vows, Tucker took both of Remi's hands in his again. "No fair, you had time to plan," she teased before he could begin, and then he chuckled and winked at her.

"I did have time to think about what I wanted to say to you under the open sky with tree lines that look as if they could reach the heavens," he began. "Remi, you came into my life at the perfect moment. I've been a fix-it man most of my life. If something is broken, I'll find a way to repair it. It's what I do. But when it was me… when I felt wrecked inside… you came along and put me back together in ways that I never imagined possible. I'm going to spend the rest of my life doing all I can to make you feel as whole and as happy as you have made me. I love you with all that I am, Remi."

Her tears were freefalling again, but she composed herself and spoke to the man standing before her, the man she would call her husband. "We healed each other. You, nor I, have given the other more or less. Neither of us has the greater need. That's what makes us who we are together. You give and I'll give. I'll take what I need from you and you will take what you need from me. Just please be with me for the rest of our lives, because I know I'll never feel this way about anyone else. I love you, Tucker Brandt. You and only you."

Epilogue

Six months later, Remi was in her office at the high school. She had counseled her last student for the day, and she was ready to go home. Throughout her pregnancy she had been hungry and tired all the time. Her belly was considerably round in the second trimester and it seemed like this baby boy inside of her was growing at a rapid rate. She and Tucker would have a son. Livy was going to have a brother.

"Remi?" Mary, the secretary for all of the counselors in the guidance department, called her name from the open doorway. Next to her stood a man, probably in his mid-twenties if Remi had to guess. She looked up from her desk at them. "Your brother is here to see you." Mary smiled wide, as if she was proud of the introduction. Remi's first thought was that she had heard her wrong. And her next one was, *I don't have a brother.*

Mary left the man standing alone in the doorway. And Remi was left to deal with this misunderstanding on her own. She stood now. And she stared for a long moment. He didn't look familiar, but yet he did. *She really needed to get more sleep.*

"Hi, I'm sorry, there must be some mistake," Remi began.

"Actually, I can explain," he spoke, and took two steps into her office before he stopped. He was careful to keep his distance, but he wanted to be heard. Remi listened. "My name is Clayton."

"Clayton? What is your last name?" Remi interjected. And the reason she was prompted to so abruptly ask him that question was his voice. The low-pitched tone of it instantly threw her back to her childhood.

"Jasper."

Remi froze. She had not seen her father in two decades. Her memories of him ceased when she was eleven years old. But yet, the image of him remained vivid in her mind. This man was obviously younger than Remi, maybe by five years, and it certainly could be possible that he was her brother. He had the same stance as Jon Jasper. His broad shoulders were slightly slumped. He had brown hair and thick eyebrows. If she stepped closer, she would be able to see if his eyes were also brown. *She didn't move.*

"Jon Jasper is my father, too," he said to Remi.

She inhaled a deep breath. Her hands were already trembling. The two of them were still separated across the room of that small office space. He hadn't moved too far from the doorway and she remained behind her desk.

"Why?" Remi asked. "Why are you here?" It's not as if she didn't believe him. What would a man have to gain by falsely claiming her as his sister? She was just shocked and confused.

"I'm sorry if I'm upsetting you," Clayton Jasper stated. Her condition was quite obvious and it had surprised him a little. The last thing he intended to do was cause her emotional stress that could affect her baby. He watched as Remi placed her hands on her round belly.

"I'm fine," she assured him, and he continued.

"I didn't know you existed until just a few days ago," Clayton admitted. "My father had some things to get off his chest before he passed."

Remi's eyes widened. "He died?"

"Yes, the day before yesterday."

Remi's mind reeled with questions. *Where had he lived? Had he stayed in one place all these years?* He obviously never missed her or had regrets about abandoning her because he didn't tell his own son about her until he was sucking in his last breath. Remi harbored mixed emotions all her life when it came to her father. Both anger and sadness were on the surface now.

"I'm sure you have questions," her brother read her mind. *Her brother. She had a brother.* "I can tell you what dad told me. It's why I tracked you down. You have a right to know."

"Wait," she interjected. "How did you find me?" She wasn't in Monticello, Indiana anymore.

Clayton smiled, and he almost appeared shy to her now. "Your Facebook profile isn't private."

She laughed a little. "Ah, one of the perks of social media." She thought of how she had searched her father's name once. *Not that she remembered if he was tech savvy or anything close to proficient.* They never owned a home computer, and cell phones were not lifelines then as they were now.

Clayton nodded, and began to tell her what he came there to say. And this time Remi waited until he was completely finished talking before she spoke. She wasn't even sure what to say after his revelation.

"Dad said that it was never his intention to leave you. He loved you, and he wanted to be a father to you. After your parents divorced, your mother told him something. Something he claimed he's not sure if he ever truly believed. He only chose to use it as a copout. He had no money for child support. He was still young enough to move on with his life, and he had met someone else — my mother," Clayton paused.

"For what it's worth, you're not going to offend me if you say something inappropriate or accusatory about my mother," Remi shook her head, "because it's probably true." Remi had spent her entire childhood defending her mother, and making excuses for her. As an adult, she inevitably chose not to do that anymore.

"In this case, I hope not," Clayton replied. "And looking at you, I see the resemblances that we share. We both look like him. Me, more so, but your deep brown eyes are the same." Remi walked around from standing behind her desk. He wasn't a threat to her. And she did want to hear all he had to say. "Your mother told him that you were not his daughter, not biologically."

Remi stood only about five feet from him now. Her face fell. "And he believed her? Just like that? No DNA tests to prove that I, in fact, was his? Or what about just trusting that we loved each other for the first eleven years of my life! My mother was a liar. My father knew that, and so did I." *Damn him for being a coward.* Remi felt instant tears well up in her eyes.

Clayton's heart went out to her. Her mannerisms as she had gone from angry to sad were very much like their father's. The Jasper genes were strong and dominant among the three of them.

"He knew. I believe that he knew you were his daughter. He never would have told me to look for you, to find you and tell you the truth."

"What good does it do him or me now? He's dead. I tried to act as if he had died throughout all those years after he left me. It was easier that way. So I guess nothing changes? Thanks for coming, Clayton."

Remi turned her back, and she damned those pregnancy hormones. She was stronger than that. She never let anyone see her pain. Not until Tucker came into her life.

Clayton stepped toward her. Her back was to him. He reached out his hand and gently placed it on her shoulder. "It's okay to hate him and love him. I did for most of my life." Remi turned. She looked into his deep brown eyes. The same as hers.

She was wrong. Something did change that day. Remi may have lost her father all over again, but she gained a brother.

ooo

Ten years later, Remi walked the path at Hidden Lake Winery on the date of her and Tucker's wedding anniversary. She closed her eyes, and felt the cool air on her face. If she stayed that way, she could imagine him there with her.

JT had walked ahead, scuffing his shoes on the path of fallen twigs the width of a pencil and dried leaves that still had their color but were blown out of the tree too soon. Remi watched him. He walked like Tucker. He was built like Tucker, already thick and robust. He was good with those strong hands. And he also had his father's kind heart, as he didn't know a stranger, and always rooted for the underdog.

He reached the end of the trail that led to the place overlooking the water where Tucker had proposed to her, where they vowed to love each other forever. JT stopped and waited.

"Tell me again, what dad did right here," JT requested of his mother. She had been telling him the story she relived in the same spot on this exact date ever since Jon Tucker was five years old.

"You were in my belly," Remi began, with a smile, "and your dad and I were walking out here before dinner. It was my first time here, and he knew I would love it. The trees were beautiful colors, just like they are now. This is where your dad asked me to marry him, and right over there," Remi pointed, "he had a minister waiting to make us husband and wife. Of course I said yes, and we were married here that day." Remi smiled again at the memory. Her heart was still full of undying love for that man. She remembered, in her vows, the words that were heartfelt and impromptu in that special moment.

Be with me for the rest of our lives, because I know I'll never feel this way about anyone else.

Her heart still ached as it was now five years since Tucker left this world. And if it hadn't been for Jon Tucker, Remi would have surrendered to the pain and sorrow and suffocating grief that life had hurled at her so unexpectedly.

Tucker had been at MidAmerica Airport, a publicly used airport co-located on the grounds of Scott Air Force Base in O'Fallon. That's where the private jet, owned by Kate and her husband, Riley, was prepared for take-off to San Diego.

Tucker had argued with Kate on the phone. *Livy was eight years old, and he was not going to allow her to fly alone!* That had been the deal when Kate eventually wanted to alternate visiting Livy in O'Fallon and bringing her back to San Diego. This particular trip, Livy was due back and Kate was ill. She was battling an ear infection and could not fly. Livy wanted to come home. She missed her dad and little brother, and her friends at school. She had already been in California with Kate for an unplanned few extra days. Tucker loathed flying, as he had only once suffered through it at Kate's insistence for their honeymoon to Cabo. Kate's parents had paid for their roundtrip, and she begged Tucker to put his fear of flying aside. For her. To celebrate the start of their life together.

Tucker had given in then, just as he gave in for Livy that day. He agreed to fly to her in California, and then turn around and fly back home with her.

Remi could still remember their last conversation. Their cell phone connection was static-filled at times as Tucker walked in the blustery wind near the runway to reach the private jet. He told himself this was not a favor from Riley Ratchford. He couldn't have cared less about what that man's money could buy. This was for his daughter. His beautiful eight-year-old little girl who was content being a family with him and Remi and little JT.

"I'm not happy about this," Tucker had told Remi on the phone. *"Livy isn't going to fly back there for awhile. Kate can fly here to her. I'm done with this craziness. Liv isn't a fan of flying either. She told me so. She only does it to appease Kate."*

"I know," Remi had said to him, pressing the phone close to her ear so she wouldn't miss a word Tucker said to her. *"You're doing this for Livy. Just be safe and come back to me soon."*

"Three hours there, three hours back," he told her. "*And Rem… when I'm up there in the clouds, I'm only going to be thinking of you."*

"I love you," she told him one last time, and he smiled into his phone. He never tired of hearing those words from her. And he never would.

"Mom!" JT interrupted her memory. Her tears were freefalling on her face again. She brushed them away with her fingers, and looked over at her son. "She's here. She made it!"

Remi glanced behind her, and down just a short way on the trail was Livy. She was thirteen now and had yet to reach the stage where she looked awkward. Her teeth were straight and perfect and didn't need braces, her complexion was clear, and her tiny slender figure was beginning to show curves. She was beautiful like her mother, and Remi never hesitated to remind her that she, too, had her father's kind heart just like her brother.

Livy reached them, and she hugged her little brother. Her eyes were on Remi though. "Hi," Livy spoke, carefully. She knew this was a hard day for her stepmother. The two of them shared much closeness when Livy was a little girl, but their relationship had hit an almost irreparable snag when Tucker died en route to Livy.

The first and only radioed call from the seasoned pilot of the private jet expressed that he was in distress. The jet crashed in a wooded area in Mascoutah, Illinois, shortly after take-off.

Remi blamed Kate for not taking responsibility for her daughter. Sick or not, she should have brought Tucker's daughter back to him.

Kate undoubtedly blamed herself. She had never loved another man like Tucker. And while she had lost him when they divorced, she continually hung onto the fact that they would always be connected by Livy. Tucker was gone. It completely destroyed Kate to know that Livy would grow up without her father, the man who clearly was her world and had always put her first.

Livy clung to her mother then, out of desperation and pity. And then she watched Kate turn to alcohol more than ever. After having had already lost one parent, Livy feared her mother's destructive path would also take her away, so she consequently chose to live in California with her.

Remi fought that decision and she pushed Kate to allow Livy to come home often, as often as she did when Tucker was alive. She needed to be with her brother. It was important to Remi to have the two of them be a constant in each other's lives. It's what Tucker would have wanted. It's also what Remi wanted for her son — and for herself. She loved that little girl as her own, for many reasons, and because she was a part of the man she loved.

"Hi sweetie," Remi spoke, as she pulled this fragile teenage girl in her arms. Tucker had been her world. She was a daddy's girl, even as she got older. Remi didn't know who was prouder. They beamed when they were together, and when one spoke of the other.

"You okay?" Livy asked, as JT turned to throw twigs in the water.

Remi nodded, as she held back the tears. "I am," she answered. "He's with us all the time. He's probably whispering in my ear right this moment that I was never a crier, so why now?" They both giggled a little. "Livy, can I tell you something?" Remi asked, because the timing seemed right. And Livy wasn't a child anymore. Livy nodded, and stayed close to Remi. "Before I met your daddy, I was all to myself. My childhood, and the letdowns after I became an adult, had led me to a place where I wanted very little to do with life, and especially with love. Who needed it? It hurt too much to love people. Then I met Tucker Brandt. He was quick to show me that I did need love. And that I needed him as much as he needed me. When we lost your dad, I was in so much pain. I cursed my life and the heartbreak that seemed to follow me. I wanted out. I wanted to be with your dad, above the clouds, far away from the pain of missing him so much that I couldn't breathe."

Livy listened raptly, and she started to silently cry. Remi reached and thumbed the tears on her face as Tucker used to always do. Livy instantly smiled at the memory of that. "You asked me if I'm okay, and I said that I am. Livs, the reason I am okay is because of that little boy over there," Remi looked in JT's direction, "and you. You and your brother were Tucker's whole world, and now you'll always be mine."

Livy threw herself in Remi's arms and held on for dear life. And then a voice behind them said, "Can I get in on that, too?" Jon Tucker stood behind them, looking boyish and strong. He would take care of those girls for the rest of his life – for his father.

about the author

I've written my share of sad stories over the years, but this one grabbed me by the throat and would not let go. *Is this a happy ending?* That's a difficult question to answer, and through my tears I said *No!* the first time I wrote and reread the ending to this story.

But life isn't always happy. We hear of the sad stories around us, and all of us at one point or another in our own lives will live through unbearable pain and sadness. I say the word "through" because we must live through and power through the agony in order to survive.

Everyone needs a reason to go on.

My hope for all of you —who have overcome sadness or continue to endure it— is for you to be okay. Let another day begin. Find your strength. Do it for the people who loved you, then and now.

As always, thank you for reading!

Love,

Lori Bell